AND THEN, AS IF HEARING ITS CUE, HER HORROR RETURNED . . .

She was at the corner of Broadway and Eighty-eighth, heading south, when the pay phone next to her went off.

And then the ringing stopped.

At the corner of Eighty-seventh, it happened again.

At Eighty-sixth, there were two. Ringing. Calling to her, unmistakably.

She hurried on.

At each corner, malevolent and all-seeing, it waited for her, charting the course of her return home, letting her know, all too well, that there was no escaping the Silence.

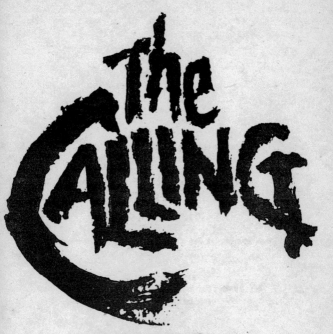

BOB RANDALL

A JOVE BOOK

This Jove book contains the complete
text of the original hardcover edition.
It has been completely reset in a typeface
designed for easy reading, and was printed
from new film.

THE CALLING

A Jove Book/published by arrangement with
Simon & Schuster, Inc.

PRINTING HISTORY
Simon and Schuster edition/September 1981
Jove edition/April 1983

ISBN: 0–515–07102–1

Jove books are published by Jove Publications, Inc.,
200 Madison Avenue, New York, N.Y. 10016.
The words "A JOVE BOOK" and the "J" with sunburst
are trademarks belonging to Jove Publications, Inc.

PRINTED IN THE UNITED STATES OF AMERICA

ACKNOWLEDGMENT

THE AUTHOR WISHES TO EXPRESS HIS GRATITUDE TO JEFFRY B. MELNICK FOR HIS GENEROUS ADVICE AND ENTHUSIASM.

FOR MICKIE

PROLOGUE

DES MOINES, IOWA, July 24, 1981—Mrs. Chazy Dowaliby of 1451 Burnes Road was reported missing last night by her husband, Vincent, who told authorities that he last saw his wife four days ago. She had been "nervous and distraught" for several weeks, according to neighbors. Her mother, Mrs. Joanna Roosevelt, of 12 Plimpton Place, was unavailable for comment. . . .

Daily Sun
Cedar Rapids, Iowa

WEST HOLLYWOOD, CALIFORNIA, July 28, 1981 —Relatives of Mrs. Thomas Geyer of North Flores Avenue phoned the police this morning to report the disappearance of the divorced mother of two. They were called by neighbors when Mrs. Geyer's children, Stacey, 9, and Joshua, 6, were seen playing in the garden of their apartment dwelling after eleven o'clock in the evening. The children had apparently been left alone for several days. . . .

Los Angeles Times
Los Angeles, California

BANGOR, MAINE, August 17, 1981—Anyone having information as to the whereabouts of Helen Belasco, wife of René Belasco, of Orono, Maine, please contact the offices of the *Daily Freeman*, extension 245. Mrs. Belasco is 37 years old, five feet four inches tall, dark hair, brown eyes. She was last seen in the vicinity of the Harbor Inn. . . .

Personal Column
Daily Freeman
Bangor, Maine

PRINEVILLE, OREGON, August 27, 1981—The sheriff's office has sent out an all-points bulletin for the apprehension of Mrs. Gary Pratt, missing from her home on Wappinger Road since last Thursday morning. Mrs. Pratt was released from the Prineville House of Detention on bail, awaiting her trial on charges of assault with a deadly weapon. The plaintiff, her sister-in-law, Miss Karin Banks, of Estacada, was recently released from St. Vincent's Hospital where she was treated for knife wounds. . . .

Portland Times
Portland, Oregon

1

Something was wrong.

Susan sat in her cubicle (the editor called it an office, but the editor called apartments "flats") and thought. The morning had gone as usual. Lou lectured aloud to himself about business over breakfast, Andrea spilled everything within her reach, and the dog, Sweet William, whimpered and finally gave up and peed on the hall floor. Business as usual.

But something was wrong.

"You want to go to Bloomie's during lunch and get ripped off?" Tara's pretty head appeared over the glass partition that separated their cubicles.

"Uh-huh."

"Good. We'll get through the day yet," and Tara sank down and was dispersed by the thick glass.

Susan felt better immediately; Tara Karsian had that effect on her. They had worked side by side (or nearly, given the thickness of the glass) for seven

months, ever since Susan had announced to Lou
("announced" was the wrong word; "whimpered"
like Sweet William?) that waiting for Andrea to get
out of school was not what her parents had sent her
to Barnard for and she wanted to go back to work.
Lou had given his "permission" (again the wrong
word. "Blessing"? Hardly. "Permission" would
have to do). And so, here she was, *en cubicle*, illustrating a group of ladies' magazines from approxi-
mately nine to somewhat before five each day. Three-
thirty was a killer—when Andrea was picked up at
school by Mrs. Diamond instead of by her mother.
Susan wondered if the blacks also felt guilt at their
liberation.

Today's work was a watercolor still life of a quiche
that would simultaneously impress company and act
as an aphrodisiac on one's husband. She mixed the
green of baked spinach.

"Are you sure Mary Cassatt started this way?" she
called to Tara's wiggling image.

"Shut up and draw," came back.

Though the job was not what she had in mind
(today a quiche, tomorrow a casserole) Tara more
than made up for it. She was a few years younger
than Susan, in her early thirties, and, wonder of won-
ders, nobody's wife and nobody's mother. With a
gun pressed to her temple, Tara would still be unable
to say an intelligible word about potty training or
secondary schools. And she had the audacity to live
in the Village instead of on West End Avenue. God
bless her.

The grass is always greener, Susan thought, and,
glancing at her brush, decided the green she had
mixed was more like backed grass than spinach.

They grabbed a bite at The Heavenly Burger, during which time Tara regaled Susan (knowing full well that she was embarrassing her) with her sexual exploits of the previous evening, centering around a man of, if you can believe it, twenty-two.

"My God!" Susan laughed.

"A body like silk," Tara added. "A mind like rayon."

"Are you going to see him again?"

"I can't avoid it. He's staying at my apartment till his father sends his allowance."

They always laughed heartily at lunches; Tara's round Armenian face would fall, chin resting on collarbone, black hair trembling, as she tried to hide her hysteria from onlookers, Susan's thinner, more angular face thrown back, the honeyed hair hanging behind her, laughing at the ceiling.

Lunches with Tara were one of the best parts of being alive and she loved her for them.

They ravaged Bloomingdale's, spending too much, as always, egging each other on, approving, disapproving, suggesting, whispering behind the salesperson's back, giddy with comradery.

And then it hit Susan.

Something was wrong.

They were in the elevator on the way back when Tara noticed it.

"What's the matter?"

"Don't know," Susan answered. "I just have this funny feeling that something's wrong."

"When's your period due?" Tara asked, much too loudly for Susan.

"Tell you what—" and Susan leaned in and whispered, "When it's our floor, I'll turn around and tell everybody I had my period last week.''

"Last week? That's great!" Tara boomed, and Susan pinched her.

The feeling persisted.

They were having dinner—their usual easygoing, sloppy dinner with Sweet William lying under Andrea's chair to catch the inevitable droppings and Lou talking non-stop with his mouth full.

". . . I told him if he'd come down five hundred we'd take it for August. Would you like that, babe?" He wiped mashed potatoes from Andrea's cheek. "You want to live next to the ocean?"

"I wanna go to camp."

"When you're ten."

"Shi—" and she thought better of it. "Shoot."

Lou glanced at Susan and realized she hadn't said a word in minutes; in a family where everyone talked and no one listened it was a dead giveaway.

"How was work?"

"Boring."

"Want to quit yet?"

"Want to shut up yet?"

"Ooh, what Mommy said!"

"How's your mother?"

"The job's fine, my mother's fine, everything's fine, Your Honor." Having a lawyer for a husband had its irritating moments. But of course this wasn't one of them and so she apologized. "Sorry. I'm just fractious today."

"Anything I can do?"

She looked at him, at his still youthful, still handsome, still sexy face and wondered why she felt the way she did. It wasn't her usual dissatisfaction with her slice of the American dream pie; this feeling was worse. Like a far-off call of danger.

"You can load the dishwasher."

"Done."

"And you can give Andrea her bath."

"Done."

"And you can stop being so nice to me when I'm being so mean to you."

"Also done." And he punched her playfully on the arm.

"That hurt," she said, scowling.

It was worse later that night.

They had made love and that part was good, but then Lou had rolled away from her and fallen asleep, just as she was preparing to tell him of her premonition or fear or whatever it was. She was chastising him to herself when Sweet William, who could always sense her upset, laid his enormous muzzle on her arm. She turned toward him and patted the bed, the signal that he could join her. He did, not nearly as gracefully as he might have a year ago, and she cradled the old dog. He whimpered, his sole sound, and she kissed his forehead and wiped away the ever-present drippings from his eyes. She had loved Sweet William for fourteen years, before Lou, before Andrea, before she had grown into whatever it was that she was. She bought him when she moved into her first apartment; he was a part of her freedom, her identity. And now he was old. She kissed him again and, suddenly overwhelmed with regret, decided to dress and take him for a walk, while she still could.

It was almost one in the morning and the avenue was deserted. Sweet William pranced at the end of his leash, thrilled by his unexpected treat. They turned the corner and started toward Riverside Drive, down the darkness of West Seventy-seventh Street. She had never liked the street, and she especially disliked it at night. It was lined either side with five-story graystones, once townhouses, then shabby rooming houses, now reconverted apartments, mostly rented by gay young men. But the look of the houses, rather than their inhabitants, was what put Susan off. They seemed, in the darkness, to be old people, gigantic old people, standing there watching, thinking, whispering among themselves about you. It was, if such a thing existed, a hostile street.

At the corner of Riverside Drive, Sweet William found his fire pump and Susan her company. A young couple languidly moving up the avenue, their arms around each other, their easy, obvious sexuality on display for all the establishment in their large expensive apartments to see, if they cared to look out their windows. Susan cared to look. She watched them saunter away and wondered: How long has it been since I was like them? How long since Lou's body was all there was?

She ached, briefly, the ache of not being young, and then Sweet William was finished and they started back toward West End Avenue.

There was a ringing.

A pay phone, up the hill almost to the corner. Ringing on the deserted street. The sound was eerie, as if an apartment had been turned inside out, ending up in front of, rather than inside, its building. There was something personal about it; something that didn't fit a deserted, hostile street at night.

"God, am I dumb," Susan said to Sweet William, and he wagged his tail in agreement.

But as she passed the phone, still ringing, Susan shuddered and quickened her pace back to their building.

Later, in bed, she wondered why she hadn't answered the phone.

But she was glad that she hadn't.

2

The omens began several weeks later.

Susan had forgotten her feeling of foreboding and had returned to her characteristic cheery self. Nothing had happened; nothing was likely to. She and Tara, both illustrating modern gothic stories (will women read absolutely *anything?*), planned to use their lunch break to cab it to the Village, to Tara's apartment, where her new wallpaper was up and begging to be appreciated. But it was another taxi that troubled Susan. Her illustration, of a typically beautiful, typically distressed young woman getting out of a cab in front of a typically ominous manor house, was going badly. The woman and the house were no problem, but Susan struggled over the taxi all morning. One rendering had it vaguely thirties, almost to the running board. In another, it was more an elongated Volkswagen than a cab. She cursed all the years she had wasted in school being *typically*

11

feminine and drawing women and clothes in her textbooks while the boys, more sensible, drew cars and planes. Finally, in desperation, she settled on a somewhat fifties Edsel look-alike and put a wash of yellow over it. It looked ridiculous, but then, her readers were no doubt as feminine as she and wouldn't notice.

"On your mark, get set, go," Tara announced over the partition, already snatching her purse and preparing to flee.

They hit the street, part of an army of midtown office workers with one thing on its collective mind: to get a cab by whatever means. They were no match for the men, who dodged traffic and caught their cabs in the middle of the gutter; nor were they any competition for the women from Bendel's, who were used to getting their way. They eventually walked over to the Warwick and waited in line like *ladies*, and eventually were rewarded with a filthy yellow heap whose meter clicked like a frantic Geiger counter.

". . . It's a kind of taupe background," Tara went on about her newest acquisition, "but not so taupe that you'd want to throw up. And the flowers are carnations and asters in coral and beige, and if you don't like it, clam up. It cost a mint. . . ."

But Susan had ceased to listen; she was studying the back of the driver's head, aware of a growing nostalgia, but for whom?

". . . I found some material at Schumacher's that's kind of the same color and I was thinking of drowning my couch in throw pillows if it wouldn't be too precious. . . ."

Brian Coleman, Susan realized. For some inexplicable reason the back of the driver's head reminded her of Brian Coleman. He had been her friend, her best friend, in elementary school. But, of course, this was not to be a chance reunion. Brian had gone off to camp one summer, had contracted spinal meningitis and died. He was the first person Susan had known who'd died. Others had followed: her father, a cousin, an elderly neighbor—but they were anti-climaxes after Brian.

". . . So what do you think?" Tara at last paused for breath.

"Huh? About what?"

"About blowing up the Coliseum."

"Sorry, I was elsewhere."

"You're telling me?"

And so Susan, the dutiful friend, entered into a conversation about pillows and curtains that lasted until the cab pulled up in front of Tara's brownstone. Then, quite by chance, she glanced at the driver's picture (why do they always look like escapees from Attica?) and his name.

Brian Coleman.

She read it twice before she felt her adrenaline hit from within.

"Excuse me," she said, "your name is Brian Coleman?"

"Yeah." He turned around and presented a stranger's face to her.

No possibility that she'd ever seen it before.

"Did you go to P.S. Six?"

"Nope."

"My name is Susan Reed . . . Goodman . . . Susan Goodman," she stammered, a little breathless from the adrenaline. "Did you ever know me?"

He raised an eyebrow at her and turned around. "Nope."

Feeling enormously foolish, Susan insisted on

paying for the cab, overtipped the driver to assuage her embarrassment, and followed Tara up the steps into the hallway of her building.

"God, Susan, he wasn't even cute," Tara said, with a wink.

The second time was a few days later.

It was Sunday, a gorgeous early-spring Sunday, and Lou had finally been dunned into taking Andrea off for the day, leaving Susan with that rarest gem in a wife/mother's crown of jewels—an afternoon alone. She spent the first hour of it struggling with the *Times* crossword, finally giving in and consulting Mr. Webster, who was little help. Then, deciding her life was truly not directly proportional to how many little boxes she could fill in, she tossed the paper aside and wondered how she might best enjoy her afternoon.

What would she have done on a beautiful Sunday years ago? Before there were Lou and Andrea and Responsibilities and Duties and Expectations?

The Frick, of course.

She purposefully chose her oldest clothes, the ones she had owned when she was single, and dressed.

She opted to walk through Central Park to heighten the enjoyment of the day.

Enjoyment was hardly the word. Ecstasy was more like it. The park was filled with celebrants, and Susan felt, if not exactly twenty again, nowhere near thirty-seven, thirty-eight, thirty-nine, bingo!

She strolled among the revelers, choosing a path that wound beside the lake, near the ball fields that would, she knew, be filled with baseball and soccer fanatics—the people who loved the city as she did.

She felt great comradery with them all, and wished them all well.

And then, near the end of the lake, a rustling of the winter's remnants of leaves up ahead, and a squirrel, more Walt Disney than real, approached her. She regretted having been so selfish in her happiness that she forgot to pack a handout.

"Sorry, sweetie," she said and walked on.

And the squirrel followed, circling her, stopping in front of her to beg.

"Would you accept a promissory note?" Susan said, utterly charmed by it.

It cocked its head.

And followed.

She was almost out of the park at the Metropolitan Museum with its hordes when she saw it again: hanging back, sadly, it seemed to her, afraid of the crowds and traffic.

She waved to it and felt silly and wonderful.

Then down Fifth she strolled, enjoying the people, not enjoying the teenagers with their blaring transistor radios, wondering how much the grand buildings across the street were charging for rent these days, noticing the shoes on the smarter women, the jeans on nearly everybody, the plethora of mustaches on the incredibly sexy young men. Would Lou look good in a mustache? Go away, Lou, she thought. This is *my* afternoon. Grow your mustache on your own time.

And then she saw the squirrel again; at least, she assumed it was the same squirrel. It was running along the stone wall directly beside her.

Looking at her.

She stopped. It stopped.

She walked on. It scampered along after her.

"Such loyalty must not go unrewarded," Susan said aloud, and that also amused her. She looked around and happily saw a vendor not half a block away. As she approached it, her squirrel, for now she felt it was *her* squirrel, hesitated, sat upright on the wall, and waited.

She bought it a pretzel, unsalted, lest it make Hobeau thirsty (that was its name, Hobeau) and approached it. It held its arms out to her and took the pretzel, transferred it to its mouth, blinked in gratitude and leaped from the wall to the bushes and obscurity, leaving Susan thrilled with the encounter.

The smell of the Frick was as she remembered it: a mixture of flowers and lemon oil, a grand, reminiscent fragrance that never failed to make her feel that special joy of the connoisseur. For though Susan could not reproduce the beauty of the paintings around her, no one in her acquaintance appreciated them more than she. She had an almost visceral reaction to a fine painting; conversely, gallery hopping in Soho invariably brought on a headache.

It was the former feeling that filled her as she stood before a Delacroix in the study of the house, trying to blank out the lecture going on beside her. A young man, impressing the girl he was with, was busily misinterpreting the intentions of the painting. There was a time he would have amused Susan; now she merely wished he'd go away and grow up.

She strolled over to a Sargent, one of her favorite favorites and floated on its grace for a moment. And then into the main gallery and the Goyas. In a very few minutes she experienced that timeless, serene sensation that always accompanied a visit to a great museum. She was an art freak, no doubt about that.

But art freak or not, time was running out. Lou and Andrea might at that moment be on their way back to the apartment, filled with needs. Susan hurried through some portraits, not minding, spent all too brief a moment before a Vermeer, and strolled into the atrium with its reflecting pool. It was several degrees cooler in there and damp. She wandered along the pool's edge, enjoying the cool, the silence, the change in the feeling of the air.

And then she saw something in the pool.

Floating.

She didn't want to look at it, but she did, and, recognizing it, she left the museum, hailed a cab and went home, depressed and out of sorts.

It was a squirrel.

The third and final omen.

Lou was inside her.

"I love you," he whispered.

"I love *you*," she answered.

A breeze from the open window blew across them, cooling them momentarily. The blinds were half up, and a mixture of moon and city lights illuminated the room. Susan made love with her eyes closed, but had she looked at the window, she would have seen the woman on the roof of the building across the street, standing there by the ledge, watching them.

"I love you," Lou whispered again and Susan clasped her hands behind his back and pulled him closer and deeper.

And the woman watched.

They made love for a long time. Lou was considerate always and tonight especially so; their lovemaking, usually good, was brilliant.

And the woman climbed up onto the ledge.

"Sweetheart . . ." Susan moaned, approaching orgasm.

"Baby . . . do it for me . . ."

Susan's cries could not possibly have carried out to the woman, who stood there at the edge of the precipice, waiting. But as they reached a crescendo, she leaped.

Later, when the police arrived and the sirens broke the silence, Susan stirred briefly and went back to sleep, still glowing.

3

The first time it happened, it had the full force of an attack, a fit.

It had been a disagreeable day to begin with. Susan's mother met her for lunch, spent the entire hour and a half trying not to complain of her loneliness and consequently made Susan feel responsible for it. Then, as if that burden weren't enough, her editor ("Call me Maudey, darling") conned her into working at home over the weekend ("It's a divine idea; you're the only one who can do it justice") even though she'd promised to spend Saturday at the Bronx Zoo with Andrea.

Susan dragged herself home at five-thirty, avoided open hostilities with Mrs. Diamond (Andrea's drill sergeant) and hit the kitchen. She was pouring out frozen french fries when the phone rang.

Weeks from then, Susan would still be unable to

verbalize how she knew there was evil on the other end of the line, but she knew.

There was no sound. Nothing. No background noise, no voice, no static, no air, no white noise.

Nothing but a presence. A despicable presence.

She listened to it, shocked.

It was as if sound and time and space had imploded. She was listening to a black hole.

Mesmerized, stunned, she took almost a minute before she spoke.

"Yes?" she said and her voice came out thick and fearladen only to be sucked into that black hole.

She hung up quickly. The entire call had lasted a little more than a minute, but as Susan came around from the shock of it, she found herself drenched in perspiration. Her hair was matted to her neck; sweat from her upper lip dripped into her mouth.

"My God," she whispered, as much to relieve her tension as to hear sounds again.

And blessedly, other sounds came to comfort her; the TV in the living room that Andrea was watching, the traffic in the streets, the shuffling of Sweet William's paws as he came into the room.

He looked at her and whined.

She became aware that she was holding tight to the counter top, holding *on*.

Sweet William, his tail drawn up between his legs, hurried to her. He pulled at her hand with his paw, pushing his face into her, whining, smelling panic.

When Susan came fully around, Sweet William was in a panic himself, pacing the kitchen, whining, peeing small puddles on the floor. Something was boiling over on the stove and she could smell gas. She turned off the stove and comforted the dog—"It's all right, it's all right, boy—" but he started to shiver and would stop only when she held him close to her. But she was shivering, too.

Lou entered the kitchen at six o'clock and, seeing Susan sitting at the table, staring at its surface, went to her.

"What's happened?" he said, instinctively putting his arms around her.

She looked up at his face, at the concern there, at the man she loved and trusted and would spend her life with, and she tried to speak.

"What is it?" he asked, tightening his grip on her, preparing both of them for the dread news that would shortly have to be dealt with.

And she wept.

Later, when she was calm, and Lou had sent Andrea next door to have dinner with friends, she tried to explain it to him.

"What do you mean, there was no sound?" he asked, relieved and perplexed.

"I don't know," she said. "I don't know!"

"Come on, honey, calm down. As far as I can tell, nothing's happened, so what're you so upset about?"

"I'm trying to tell you, something *did* happen."

"What?"

"There was somebody there! There was some *thing!*"

They went on for almost an hour before Susan, exhausted and unable to explain her terror, went into their bedroom and lay down. Lou, confused, felt the beginnings of fear for her (not of any *thing* on the phone, but of what Susan was making of it) and, unable to help in any other way, started to prepare dinner.

Susan didn't imagine it. She didn't. She didn't.

She sat up in bed and lit a cigarette. There *was* something there. There was!

Lou came into the room (after three cigarettes had been lit and prematurely crushed) carrying a wicker tray.

"It's insult-to-injury time," he said, smiling weakly. "My cooking."

She was in his arms as soon as he put the tray on the night table.

"I can't explain it, Lou. I just know something terrible happened."

"Maybe it did. . . ."

"It did!"

"But it's over now. You're here and I'm here and even the dog has shut up. Can't you calm down?"

"I want to."

"Let me help." He kissed her, the kiss that had eased all sorts of pain out of her for eleven years, but this time it failed.

"I'm better now," she lied, out of gratitude, but was immediately resentful when he released her.

"Hungry?" he asked.

"No."

"You'll feel better if you eat."

"You're Catholic. You're not supposed to talk like that."

"I've been living with a Jew for a long time. It's catching."

She meant to smile at that, he deserved a smile, but she couldn't.

In a little while Andrea came hollering into the apartment and life returned to a semblance of normalcy. But Susan knew she would spend many days waiting. Waiting for it to happen again.

And it would.

* * *

"It's the damndest thing I ever heard," Tara said the next morning. "Real 'Twilight Zone.' "

"I know." Susan finished her coffee. "I don't even know how to explain it. It was just so . . . horrifying."

"Jesus."

"Don't tell anybody, huh?"

"Why not? I was just about to get on the phone."

"Because it sounds so stupid. Everybody'll think I'm on drugs or something."

"Hey, there's an explanation. You on drugs or something?"

"Oh, shut up."

"Listen, if you can't fight it, joke about it."

But Susan didn't feel like joking about it. She went back into her cubicle and tried another defense: work. After two hours, she had sketched out a Thanksgiving dinner party that was a cross between Norman Rockwell and Edward Hopper. She used her father's face (as he had been before his death) on the man behind the turkey, and her mother's (the worry lines removed, the mouth lifted from its now characteristic droop) on the proud woman at his side. And there she was, Susan at twelve, sitting at the table expectantly. Beside her, the brother she had never known, who had been miscarried a year before her birth. This brother, the one she had often felt love and guilt for, was reaching across the table, grabbing at biscuits, while a grandmother (a fabrication—Susan had never seen either of hers) scolded him. And there, behind the table, waiting for scraps, Sweet William, who had whined far into the night. She studied the sketch for a long time, taking calm from its serenity, adding touches, a bottle of catsup (she mistakenly gave it the 1920s Campbell's label), an apron for her mother, freckles on her brother. It had not been like that, really. Her parents were not truly happy together, no matter how vociferously her mother mourned her husband's passing. There was, of course, no brother, no grandmother, just a series of tedious aunts and uncles who complained a great deal about each other. And no dog. Her father had squelched all pleadings for one, saying that dogs had to be walked ("I'll do it! I'll do it!" she had implored to no avail) and messed up an apartment. Of course, he was right—she remembered cleaning up Sweet William's puddles that morning. But there, in her own sketch, were all her nearly forgotten longings: for the closeness, the gaiety, the security. Once denied, they were denied for good. Not even Lou and Andrea could touch that secret scar.

Susan felt melancholy; it was a good feeling, an honest one, unlike the imagined panic of the night before. (Imagined or real, what difference did it make? Lou was right. Nothing had changed. She'd had a bad time, but it was over. Now, to forget it.)

"Hey, Mrs. Rembrandt," Tara called over the glass, "you wanna cut out?"

"I don't think so." Susan stared at the sketch. "I think I'll work through lunch."

"Like I said, are you on drugs or something?"

"Bring me back a sandwich, will you?"

"Dainty tuna or liberated roast beef?"

"Middle-of-the-road chicken salad."

She worked the outlines of the sketch in ink, carefully, taking enormous pride in her pains. And then the base colors and shadings and textures. It was shaping up beautifully. Had she honestly been Rockwell or Hopper, she couldn't have felt more pleasure at her task. The re-creation of her childhood—done right this time. Done with love and peace. No subterranean angers. No silences filled with resentments. No dead babies.

"Myself, I think chicken salad is too noncommittal," Tara said, plopping the bag too close to the wet gouache.

Susan had been working for almost two hours and hadn't felt the slightest passage of time.

"Hey, that's nice." Tara studied the picture casually. "But where's the cat and the priest?"

The phone on Susan's drawing board rang.

"Jesus," Tara said, seeing her reaction, "relax, will you?" She picked it up. "Susan Reed's line. . . ." Susan studied her face anxiously. "Hi 'ya, handsome . . . yeah, she's here. Hold on." She handed the phone to Susan. "I don't hear a thing."

"Bitch." And Susan accepted it.

It was Lou, suggesting they meet after work and have dinner out. He'd already checked with Mrs. Diamond and she'd be delighted with the extra money.

"How come?" Susan asked.

"I hate your cooking."

"And my carrying on?" And she realized how ungrateful that sounded. "Thanks, honey, I'd love to. I'll meet you in the lobby at five-thirty."

"How will I recognize you?"

"I'll be the calm one."

She hung up, and Tara, half out the door, said, "It isn't concern, it's guilt. We're having an affair."

"The hell you are. Your complexion isn't that good."

"And you call *me* a bitch?"

*　　*　　*

They dined at the Fleur De Lis, a small West Side restaurant whose duck in cherry sauce had served them well in the past for minor reconciliations and celebrations. This time, Susan thought ruefully, it was a bribe—the kind one might offer a child to behave. Nonetheless, she was grateful. It was only recently that her consciousness had been raised (damn that phrase) to the point of recognizing Lou's condescension to her, but resentment hadn't yet built up and anger was far off. It was with a clinical acceptance that she realized she and Lou were part of a now, to be hoped, dying breed: the strong man and the little woman. But he *was* strong, and she felt, at that moment, very little indeed.

They had martinis, always a sign that giddiness was not far off, and she felt, as she had when working on the Thanksgiving sketch, a release of tension.

"Hey, we haven't played the game in ages," Lou said, almost finished with his second drink. "I think it's your turn."

The game had started years before and consisted of fantasizing aloud to each other; building their dream homes and careers and life style. It was more than a game, though. It helped them tell each other, through daydreams, where they were.

"Yeah? What was I up to?" Susan swirled her olive and noticed how absolutely lovely its shape was.

"You were decorating the solarium in the country house."

"Ah, yes, dear old Ravenhurst. Well, I think the floor should be tiled. White tiles, pure and pristine . . ."

"With little yellow stains from the dog."

She cocked her head at him, realizing something. "Why do you always call Sweet William 'the dog'? He's got a name. Do you call me 'the wife' when I'm not around?"

"No, I call you 'the punishment.' "

"Very funny."

"It was intended to be."

She scowled. "I shall continue. The walls will be white stucco, the furniture wicker, not new wicker, old wicker from the twenties with some personality to it, the upholstery green, with flowers . . . oh, shit, I never called your mother back."

"Flowers remind you of my mother?"

"No, upholstery. She wants to buy us a bedspread."

"Yeah? What's wrong with our old bedspread?"

"She didn't give it to us."

Their duck arrived and aborted the game, but it was over, anyway, or soon would be, for Susan was not enjoying it. You couldn't insult Sweet William and expect his mistress to remain in the mood to play.

Soon Lou wandered to the subject of his work, as always, and told Susan a mildly interesting story about a writer client who was thinking of suing his producer, who was thinking of suing the writer, and Susan drifted off into her own thoughts.

She was back in the solarium, carefully examining swatches for the chairs. The sun was pouring in through the glass walls, the rosebushes outside were astonishing, Andrea and Sweet William were cavorting on the lawn, her first one-woman show had sold out, she had accepted a commission to do a mural on the facade of the State Theater, her breasts had suddenly lifted to their previous contour. Why can't life be like that? Why is it when you get what you want (Lou, Andrea, the job) it's never enough? What more is there, anyway?

Susan was about to feel guilty (for possibly the hundredth time that week) when the check arrived.

"I'll pay," she said, reaching for it.

"Don't be silly." Lou glanced at the waitress who held back a step from the table.

"It's not silly. I work, too."

He didn't argue the point, but as Susan withdrew two twenties from her purse and put them on top of the check, Lou said, "If you let me charge it, I can deduct it."

"Deduct this." And she held up the middle finger of her left hand.

Lou was not amused, but the waitress was.

They strolled up Broadway, arms around each other, loose, warm, a little high still, looked in shop windows, played another of their games (if-you-had-to-live-with-something-in-the-window-for-life, what-would-it-be?) and generally enjoyed themselves. There were a lot of people to look at on the streets: old women in out-of-date clothes, young people hurrying to and from sex, beautiful exotics, tawdry welfare-hotel dwellers, streetwise New York children. Could anyone possibly want to live anywhere else? Was there anywhere else?

They arrived home a little after nine. Lou paid Mrs. Diamond, Susan checked on Andrea, who was snoring to beat the band, and she remembered that she was not only a mother but a daughter-in-law. She went into their bedroom to call Lou's mother.

It was there.

As she lifted the receiver, she heard it.

The implosion. The evil. The threat.

"Lou!" she screamed with such force that he ran into the room.

"What?"

She pointed at the phone, which now lay on the bed, having dropped from her hand as if it were molten.

At first he looked at her, not understanding, and then suddenly he did, and he grabbed the receiver. He held it to his ear as Susan backed away.

"Do you hear it?" she whispered.

Lou looked at her and on his face was a hint of the panic she felt.

After a moment, he spoke. "Honey, it's just a dial tone."

4

Despite herself, Susan compared Lou and Tara.

In the next few days, as Susan grew tight and wary (the ringing of a phone, any phone, would frighten her), Lou tried to help, but his male rationality lead quickly to disbelief, and then, most degrading of all, to solicitousness. Tara, however, was there, believing it all, eyes wide with honest concern, even becoming angry that anyone or anything would so upset her friend.

They called the phone company (Tara dialed). That was supremely hopeless.

". . . Madam, are you reporting a dead phone?"

"No, I'm trying to explain to you—" Susan took a deep breath and repeated herself once more— "There's a sound on my phone . . ."

"What kind of a sound, madam?"

"I don't know; I can't describe it! A dreadful . . ."

"Would you like to speak with my supervisor? I'm

31

sorry but there's really very little I can do. If you want the phone removed . . ."

And so Susan spoke to the supervisor and that was worse.

Then, one morning at the office, Tara had the answer.

She entered Susan's cubicle, lowered herself heavily, as she always did, on the drawing board and gloated. "Don't thank me. A small token from Tiffany's main floor will do."

Susan looked up from disloyal thoughts of Lou. "What shouldn't I thank you for?"

"I think I've got your phone problem licked."

"What?"

"I think I know what's been going on, and boy, is it something!"

Susan recognized Tara's tone; she was going to stall, better to enjoy her moment of glory.

"What is it?"

"You know my friend Joan Petrowsky? The one who's got the antique shop?"

"Yes?"

"Well, last night I was at her apartment with a few of the Village dingbats. Jack, that guy I introduced you to at . . ."

"Tara, don't give me a guest list, just tell me what you're talking about!"

"Joan's had the same thing."

Susan felt a premature welling up of relief—if someone else had experienced the fear, then it was real, explainable!

"She's heard that noise?"

"Yup. Well, not exactly, but it's the same thing, at least the way Yuri explained it . . ."

"Who's Yuri?"

"I thought you didn't want a guest list."

"Please." Susan laughed. "You're toying with a woman's sanity!"

"Okay, I'll get to the point, but you owe me one. Yuri Gross was one of the guys at Joan's . . ."

"One of the dingbats."

"Not this one. He's an associate professor at the University of Haifa who came over here to do some research at NYU and, between you and me, to screw every American girl he can get his hands on, I've got a date with him tonight, anyway—" she took a quick breath—"I told everybody about your experience, I know you told me not to, but I didn't mention your name and if I hadn't told them, we wouldn't have found out what was going on . . ."

"Simple declarative sentences, please!"

"Don't nudge me, I'll work cheaper. Anyway—" and Tara paused for dramatic effect, which irritated Susan—"Joan started telling about an experience she had with the phones and pretty soon everybody was adding their two cents and then Yuri took over. God, he's a hunk. Guess what his field is?"

"If you don't get to the point, I'm going to stab you with a Magic Marker."

"Extrasensory perception. That's not what he calls it, but that's basically it. You know, psychic phenomena, telekinetics . . ."

"Oh, shit, Tara," Susan said, turning away, the disappointment sharp.

"Don't 'oh, shit' me, Susan. The man has degrees coming out of his ears, and you know how many people like you he's interviewed in the past few weeks? Hundreds! They're lined up all the way to Eighth Street and each and every one of them has had an experience that scared the hell out of them and can't be explained. Not in the usual way . . . ."

"ESP," Susan muttered to herself, taking up her brushes to wash them.

"Susan, every major university in the world is working their asses off studying ESP. Now maybe they didn't make a big deal about it in *art* school—" and she made the word sound arch—"but the rest of the world is pretty damn interested."

"God, Tara, a psychic?"

"He's not a psychic, for crying out loud. He's a professor. A scientist. Look—" and it was obvious that Tara was losing patience with Susan—"either there's an explanation for what happened to you, a good solid explanation, or you're going out of your mind, right?"

"The thought had occurred to me," Susan answered sardonically.

"Well, we both know you're too mean to go crazy, so that leaves us with trying to find out what's happening, right?"

"Right," Susan begrudged. "So?"

"So you show up at my place tonight at seven-thirty and talk to Yuri. Then, when it's all settled and there's nothing to be afraid of, you get out of there and leave us alone. God, what a hunk!"

"What's he going to do?"

"To you or to me?"

"I'm dying and you're making jokes."

"You're not dying. He's just going to talk to you. I don't know. But one thing I do know is he wasn't the least surprised or scared over what happened."

"Sure, it didn't happen to *him*."

"I'm gonna smack you soon, girl."

Susan put her arms around Tara, felt the warmth of her ample body, thanked God for her and said,

"If this doesn't work, will you go to a voodoo doctor with me?"

"That did it." And Tara smacked her bottom.

She didn't want to tell Lou.

It wasn't that she was angry with him, *exactly*. But the night before, when she mentioned her fear, he tried to erase it by making love to her, and the odd humiliation of it still lingered.

"Do you mind if I go out tonight for a while?" she asked casually, reaching over to cut Andrea's lamb chop.

"Where to?"

"Just to Tara's. Girl stuff. Don't eat that, honey. It's fat."

"But I like it."

"I know. Spit it out."

"Okay, but don't be late."

"Yes, *mein Führer*. Come on, Andrea, out with it."

The first lie between us, Susan thought, sitting there eating silently. But, of course, it wasn't. There had been a parking ticket that went undiscussed, a guilt-induced expensive present for her mother that was never agreed to, and even the classic headaches when Lou wanted to make love *at*, rather than *with*, her.

At seven, Susan made a fuss over Andrea ("Who's the prettiest girl in the world?"), dutifully put up a pot of coffee for Lou and left the apartment.

Yuri Gross was indeed a hunk.

As Susan entered Tara's small living room (two throw pillows were already on the couch with more to come; they did look precious), she tried to hide her surprise at seeing him. Tara called nearly every man a hunk, but this one, sitting there in jeans and a bulky knit sweater, was the real thing. His curly blond hair was in disarray, as if he'd just stepped off the kibbutz to check for snipers, his pale-blue Sabra eyes could cut clean through the dark of a desert night, or a woman, his hands, huge, larger than Lou's, seemed at once capable of great damage and gentleness.

Susan was surprised to find that she was blushing. Happily, Tara took it to mean discomfort with the subject to come, and so didn't push it. They had drinks and spoke amiably (his accent, too, was riveting) of the differences between Israel and America, of the Mideast, movies, whatever. And then Yuri (could he, too, have been anxious to be alone with Tara?) broached the subject.

"Tara tells me you've had an experience."

"I suppose you could call it that," Susan answered, pouring herself another needed glass of wine.

"Tell me about it," he demanded, and although the demand was made gently, it did unnerve her.

She tried to tell it calmly, almost matter-of-factly, lest he think her a hysteric and withdraw whatever help he might give. She succeeded all too well, for Tara interrupted at one point. "Jesus, Susan, tell the man how frightened you were."

"Terrified," she admitted.

"Don't be," Yuri said, and as if on command, Susan was comforted.

When she had described the sound (lack of sound) a dozen ways ("It's not like anything on earth; it's as if it were coming from another place, no place, a horrible place. . . .") Susan looked into Yuri Gross's ice-blue eyes (which never wavered) and asked, "What is it?"

"What do you think it is?" he asked, and she thought of the analyst she'd seen for two years. He, too, had answered questions with questions.

"I don't know." And she looked to Tara for some sort of support.

Tara gave it. "Whatever it is, it's scared the hell out of her."

There was a silence then, while Yuri stretched his immense, capable hands in front of him, cracked his knuckles, and thus, having introduced the seriousness of what was to follow, started.

"Have you ever heard of precognition?"

It was going to be as Susan feared, useless.

"Yes," she answered but the weariness of her reaction came through despite her intention of hiding it.

"You'll have to give up the pleasure of cynicism, just for a little while, okay?" he said, reading her perfectly.

She blushed for a second time. "I'm sorry. Yes, I think I know what precognition is."

"Hey," Tara interrupted, "what about us guys in the bleachers?"

"Think of movies," Yuri explained, and Susan recognized an edge of the same condescension Lou used on her. "The technique of flashback is old and accepted, but now there's a new technique, the flash-ahead—when a character or the audience sees, for a moment, something yet to happen. It's a familiar technique . . ."

"Gotcha," Tara said.

". . . Based on actual case histories. Thousands of them. All verified. Nothing unusual about them anymore."

"You mean psychics, right?" Susan asked.

"No, not at all. At least not professional psychics

or even amateurs. No, these are ordinary people, ordinary cynics.'' And he smiled at Susan, a dazzling if superior smile. ''People all over the world are having these experiences. They probably always have, but now that our field is recognized, they report them. People see coming calamities before they happen, happy events, even things as petty as new boyfriends—'' he looked at Tara, who said, ''You call that petty?''

He laughed and casually stroked her arm. (Yes, he was anxious for them to be alone.)

''You think that's what happened to me?'' Susan asked, hoping that the grain of acceptance she was feeling would mount into belief.

''Possibly.''

''What am I seeing . . . hearing?''

''It could be anything. An illness, death . . .'' and he saw the fright flash across Susan's face. ''Something that needn't happen for thirty or forty years.'' Her face relaxed. ''There are no time limits on precognition.''

''But I've never had an . . . experience before.''

''Of course you have. We all have. But we're not trained to recognize them and so we discount them. How's your woman's intuition?''

''Not bad, how's yours?'' Tara kidded.

''That's precognition of a socially acceptable kind. All it really means, all precognition really means, is the ability to tune in on possible eventualities, not to harden oneself into the here and now at the cost of one's full faculties. Animals do it all the time. Have you ever seen a herd of antelope before a storm? They're all over the place. . . .''

''You know, we were saying just the other day, the next time we get in a herd of antelopes, we've got to check the weather forecast.'' Again Tara lightened the mood.

"Shut up, you," Yuri said good-naturedly, running his massive hand over her face.

"You think that's it?" Susan willed her resistance down.

"Actually?" Yuri paused. "No."

"No?" She was disappointed.

"Not with two hearings. No, frankly I think what happened to you is far more commonplace."

"Aw, shit," said Tara.

"What?"

"It's what actors call sense memory." Again Susan noticed the condescension. "We have another term for it, but it doesn't matter. Simply, what it is—I'll give you an example—" and he pointed a giant index finger at Susan, who felt the impulse to bite it. "Have you ever been walking down the street and heard a song coming from someone's radio only to be strongly reminded of another time you heard the song? So strongly reminded that all sorts of things came back to you that you'd long since forgotten?"

"*Déjà vu.*" Susan was pleased that, for a moment, at least, she could stop playing the uninformed child to his smug teacher.

"Right. I think the probability is that that's what happened to you. Some sound the phone gave off, some tone, registered in your ear and you ceased hearing the phone and started hearing another sound, the memory of another sound. Something from a long time ago."

"The sound of *what?*"

"Have you had your tonsils out?"

"What?"

"Have you?" His gentle, reassuring smile came close to infuriating Susan.

"Yes."

"It could be the sound of being under ether. If you want to get romantic about it, it could be the sound of being in your mother's womb. There's a lot of evidence that the sense memory of prenatal months is enormously important . . ."

He went on. And on. And in a little while he sounded to Susan exactly like Lou, lecturing her out of her fear.

But, miraculously, it worked.

By the time Yuri ground to a halt ("The one thing you should keep in mind is that whatever you experienced, it holds no threat. It's no harbinger of doom"), Susan felt enormously relieved, grateful, resentful and attracted to him.

It was this last feeling that made her leave rather abruptly, saying to Tara at the door, "He's gorgeous, but keep your dukes up."

In the cab going uptown, she started to smile—the first genuine smile she'd had in days.

5

She was given one week's peace.

Near the end of it, exhilarated from the belief that she would never again hear the silence, and that she had indeed had a psychic experience (which was harmless) Susan threw a dinner party. Lou (she had decided he was wonderful again) helped with the cooking (Paella Valenciana, their specialty). Andrea was allowed to show off for a limited time, then trotted off to bed, and Susan settled down in the warmth of the company of friends.

Dillon Roberts, fiftyish, white-haired, British actor and raconteur, was holding forth, to the delight of everyone except his wife, Berte, on the subject of poltergeists, brought on by Susan's retelling, for the umpteenth time that week of her experience.

". . . It was in a small hotel in Cheswick, pronounced without the 'w' for those interested in things Anglophile . . .''

41

"God, Dillon, get on with it," Berte said almost good-naturedly.

". . . A cousin of mine, whom I hardly speak to, though that has nothing whatever to do with the story either, was staying overnight with her new boyfriend, a very cut-and-dried kind of chap, not one given to fancies— What was his name, dear?"

"Alfred Lord Tennyson," Berte, a German, answered, looking first to heaven and then to Susan. "If anyone has to go to work in the morning, we'll forgive you if you don't stay around for the rest of Dillon's story," and everyone chuckled.

"That's enough out of you," Dillon said. "You lost the war, now you'll have to endure my stories."

"Reparations," Berte quipped.

"At any rate, it was in the middle of the night when things started popping. The drawers in a large Queen Anne highboy slammed open and shut, open and shut, for several minutes, leaving my cousin and her beau, Richard Woodburn, that was his name, his family was in prosthetic appendages, I thought he quite suited my cousin actually, at any rate, it left them quite shattered, literally. . . ."

"How do you like that for a sentence?" Berte asked Tara, who applauded.

"And in the morning, when they told the concierge about it, she said matter-of-factly, 'Didn't anyone tell you about it before you took the room?' It seems it happened every night, the same highboy, the same drawers. No one took much notice of it, though there had been a small mention in the local newspaper and someone had come round to examine it—I suppose for poltergeist holes. Like boring worms, I expect."

"Or boring people," Berte, never one to miss an opportunity, said.

"I may be many things, my dear, but I am never boring."

"And I am Marie of Romania."

Susan laughed and it occurred to her that their friends were probably among the most delightful people to be found—another reason for exhilaration. She went into the kitchen, followed by Paul Rausch, to put up coffee.

"They're such characters," Paul said, coming up behind her.

Susan moved aside swiftly, knowing full well that Paul was about to make one of his minipasses at her. "Annie looks great," she said, bringing his wife, at least verbally, into the room with them.

"So do you."

"Thank you, sir." And Susan walked a wide circle around him to the coffee canister.

"Do I still make you nervous?"

"Uh-huh." And she widened the circle back to the stove.

"I'm never going to stop trying, you know."

"I was beginning to suspect that."

"At least I flatter you, don't I?"

"Yup."

"And who knows, someday your resistance may let down."

"Stranger things have happened; we're trading with Red China."

Annie Rausch, never a fool, at last arrived, and in a moment Susan found herself alone, counting out the spoonfuls of coffee.

The phone rang.

She picked it up without hesitation and only after a few minutes of speaking with her mother (who was, predictably, lonely and blue) did Susan realize it hadn't occurred to her that the silence might be on the other end of the line. She was finally rid of it. She plugged in the percolator and rejoined her friends, settling down next to Tara, who was arguing with Berte over Woody Allen's new movie.

And on Washington Square, in Yuri Gross's darkened laboratory, a sheet of paper on which he had made notes on Susan's experience blackened beyond reading.

6

It had a sense of humor, this thing.

Why else would it have chosen that particular moment to attack again?

It was Wednesday evening and they had gone to see *Morning's at Seven* with Dillon and Berte. It was intermission, and as they stood jammed in the theater lobby, Dillon was again holding forth.

"I quite like Elizabeth Wilson. It's a vague quality not without an underlying sarcasm . . ."

"Thank you, John Simon." And Berte, dismissing the men, turned Susan around to face her. "Are you or are you not taking a house in Seaview this summer? Because if you are, we're definitely available as house guests. I'll even muzzle Dillon."

"I suppose we are," Susan answered, glancing at her watch.

"Well, if you don't, let me know. I'll be nice to someone else."

It was a little past Andrea's bedtime, her usual bedtime, and Susan wondered if Mrs. Diamond (who of late was more interested in watching television than in caring for Andrea properly) had put her to bed yet.

"I'm going to call the baby sitter," she said and moved away from the others.

"David Rounds has an interesting quality. Rather like . . ." She was not at all disappointed to miss the rest of Dillon's review.

Downstairs in the lounge several other concerned mothers of young children waited in line for the sole phone. How predictable we all are, Susan thought. And then, a side business occurred to her: Mothers' Helpers. A woman, stationed in the lobby of each theater, would take your number and children's names. At intermission, she would call your house for you, harangue the children, browbeat the sitter, leaving you to have that precious cigarette upstairs while noticing what everyone was wearing. At twenty-five cents a mother, it might be lucrative.

". . . No, we're going out for supper after," the woman in front of her was pleading with her offspring for clemency. "Josh, I want you in bed *now*, and don't hassle me! I told you, we're going out for supper. You had your supper. It's our turn now. . . ."

Someday, Susan thought, Andrea will be a grown, lovely woman whose mother is one of the centers of her life. We will gambol, hand in hand, through Bergdorf's and Sloan's, clucking merrily as we go. And then she remembered her own bimonthly lunches with her mother and decided grown up was quite enough to ask for.

"When do they get reasonable?" the woman asked Susan as she hung up.

"My mother's still waiting," Susan answered and they shared a sisterly laugh.

Susan put a dime in the coin slot and dialed.

As she brought the receiver to her ear, it was waiting for her.

Dead. Deformed. Inside out.

She stared at the blackness of the surface of the phone, listening to the blackness within it. Her head shot back, away from the receiver, and from her throat came a growl.

She forced the receiver back in its cradle and went quickly into the ladies room as a man stood watching her and wondering whether to tell the usher he thought she was about to have a seizure.

Inside, at a sink, she washed her face with cold water and, shivering, became aware that others were in there, watching her.

She went into a booth and sat down.

Déjà vu.

She searched her purse for a handkerchief with which to dry herself.

Precognition. Harmless.

She held her face in her hands and felt her heart beat as if it were a literal pounding on her chest.

Then there *was* a pounding. Susan opened her eyes. Someone was knocking on the door of the booth. Thus humiliated, she stood up and opened the door. It was the ladies room attendant, sent for.

"Are you all right, miss?" Behind her two other women stood watching, at a safe distance. "Are you all right?"

She felt soiled and abused. She wanted to tell them

she hadn't done anything to deserve it; all she did was to try to call her child.

"Yes," she answered and closed the door on them. *What was it?*

It happened again. The next morning.

Lou had just left the apartment with Andrea (it was easier for him to drop her off at school) and Susan was busily dressing when it started.

She stared at the phone, not daring to answer it, not daring to move, hands frozen on the button on her blouse.

She counted the rings. When the twentieth one sounded (it felt as though she had been standing there immobile for a half hour) she went to the phone. She held the receiver far from her and slowly brought it closer. When it was about a foot from her, she heard it.

The obscenity.

She slammed the receiver down quickly.

"Why are you doing this to me?" she screamed at the machine, and, as if in response, it started to ring again.

"What do you want from me?"

The ringing stopped, and outside on the street a police siren went off. (Presentment? Premonition? Flash ahead? Omen?)

And again.

She wanted desperately to speak with her former analyst. She thought about it all morning at the office and then, at lunch (she begged off a previous commitment to Tara), sitting in a crowded luncheonette, she decided she would.

It wasn't that she suspected the calls were in her imagination; they were brutally real, she knew that. But there was no one she could talk to about them; Lou was sympathetic but condescending, and whether he believed her at all was still very much in question. Tara listened but couldn't fathom Susan's upset (she and Yuri had been going together for two weeks by then and she was completely under his thumb; Yuri said not to worry and so that was that). She had tried to tell Berte, who was completely mystified and refused to think of it as anything but a prank. She had even, for one foolish moment, mentioned them to her mother, who countered with the fact that no one, including her own daughter, ever called her. (That would have been funny at another time.)

And so, not wishing to wait until she returned to the office, lest she change her mind, Susan went to the pay phones in the rear of the restaurant.

And hesitated.

It is not possible, she reminded herself, to live in this world at this time and not use telephones. No matter how much one fears them. No matter how crippling their attacks.

She lifted a receiver and heard a dial tone. It was necessary to call information for his number; it had long since gone out of her memory. She felt a familiar flush of embarrassment at speaking his name to the operator (as if that in itself were an admission of something) and got the number. It had been years since she'd used it, but her finger quickly hit the buttons, as if well practiced.

She was embarrassed. To see him again meant failure. At their last meeting he had been careful to remind her that, should she need him again, he would be there. She'd laughed at that and told him that she was finally a *grownup* and could deal with her problems as one. She knew it was arrogance, but she needed arrogance to break her growing dependence on him. And, of course, she and Lou simply couldn't afford the luxury of a paid parent any longer.

The phone rang and Susan pictured it ringing in his office with the leather couch and peculiar paintings (exclusively cubist; "*Gestalt* art" she had always called it, so that he would know she was bright, though troubled).

"Peter Steinman," his voice, the same voice, said.

Susan hesitated for a moment, feeling that she was about to betray herself, and said, "Peter?" (as a sign that she was indeed not a person to dismiss, she had always called him by his first name). "It's Susan Reed."

"Susan," his old voice came back immediately with what sounded like genuine enthusiasm. "How great to hear from you!"

"Not so great, Peter. I'm in trouble."

Now a pause, and his voice darkened. "Do you want to see me?"

"Please." She hated the sound of it, and so she amended, "If you have the time."

"Do you want to come over now?"

She didn't think it would be that simple, and so she hesitated. "Yes, if you don't mind."

"Fine, but I've moved. Got a pencil and paper?"

"Yeah, just a sec, Peter." She cradled the phone between her shoulder and cheek and searched her purse for a pen. Nothing. "Could you hold on? I'll get one."

"Sure."

She placed the receiver on a small shelf below the phone and went to the cashier, who grudgingly loaned her a stub of pencil as if it were an antique of incredible value.

"I'm back," she said, picking up the phone.

It was waiting for her.

This time, despite the unexpectedness of it, she did not panic. The same sickening fear, the numbness, the thick despair were there in her, but she did not panic.

She hung up the phone quickly.

It was standing between her and Peter, this evil, not permitting her to reach out to him, to get help, to be rid of it.

As if plotting against a reasoning adversary, Susan stood there in the rear of the restaurant, forcing herself to calm, forcing herself to reason.

She had to call him again.

But the obscenity would not permit it.

Would not permit *her*.

She stopped a young man who was passing.

"Excuse me, would you do me a favor?"

He immediately saw the desperation on the woman who had touched his arm and was holding it still.

"Yeah?"

"Would you dial a number for me and give someone a message?"

He didn't answer.

"It's all right, really."

"Why don't you dial it yourself?" He was aware that she was still holding his arm.

"Please!"

He looked at her, perceived no threat to himself

and, with a shrug, agreed.

He dialed the number (Susan would not touch the phone) and got Peter's address for her. She thanked him sincerely, but, having been forced to do it, he only wanted to be rid of her, and he walked away in the midst of her thanks.

Peter's waiting room, in the basement of his newly acquired brownstone on West Ninety-third Street, was remarkably similar to his old one, in an apartment around the corner. And indeed, the furnishings were the same. The same personality-less Naugahyde chairs and couch, the tacky mar-proof tables, even the magazines (*New York, National Geographic, Natural History*) were unchanged.

It was like walking back into another time—a time when Andrea was newly born and Susan overwhelmed with a sense of loss, of hopelessness. But Peter had been quick to understand that (a cliché; postpartum depression). What would he make of this?

She reminded herself, sitting there on the squeaky club chair, that this was not her fault. This was happening to her, not because of her.

Peter came out of his office, the same, now in his fifties but the same, bungled an attempt at a smile (should he? shouldn't he?) and led her inside.

"You're looking well," he said, taking his seat as he had a hundred times before.

"I look like hell," she answered, "and with good reason." And without stopping to tell him how he looked, Susan let her troubles spill out, very much like, she realized, a child who has been sitting in grief waiting for its mother. She told him of the calls, of Lou's reaction, and Yuri's, of her own sense of impending disaster. And to her surprise, Peter's first reaction was not at all clinical.

"Have you called the police?"

It was so simple, so logical, it made her laugh.

"Why not?"

"I don't know. It never occurred to me."

"Well, before you put out a psychic shingle, shouldn't you find out if it's happening to other people?"

"I suppose, yes."

There was a momentary pause. Peter's brow wrinkled and he said, "Susan, why did you come to see me?"

She recognized the question beneath the question; she had heard it many times from him. He was asking if there wasn't something else, something she didn't want to admit.

"No, Peter," she said, and for old times' sake, she took his hand. "I'm not imagining any of it."

He smiled. "I didn't think you were."

They spoke for the rest of the forty-five minutes (over a dollar a minute, Susan remembered, ashamed) about other possibilities (other than premonitions, which Peter seemed silently to scorn). He told her, as gently as he could, about physical disorders that can cause aural hallucinations, the abusive use of drugs (she promised that was not the case), glandular dysfunction, even something called cranial reverberations.

"You mean the sound is coming from inside my head," Susan said.

"Could be."

"If I could believe that, I'd throw a party."

"Just make sure you invite me," Peter said, glancing at the bookcase clock, seeing that another patient was waiting.

They stood up and shook hands warmly.

"I'd call the police first," he said. "Then, if you want, I can put you in touch with a good neurologist, just to be sure. Meanwhile, call me next week?"

She resisted the urge to hug him but did so verbally. "You know in all this, I haven't even asked you how you are."

"Fair to middling."

"How's . . . Elaine?" She recalled his wife's name.

Peter's face registered discomfort and he was slow to answer.

"Elaine disappeared about a year ago."

She didn't return to the office but, solaced by Peter's calm, decided to walk home (how often he'd advised her to please herself), down Columbus Avenue, past and through the antique shops, the second-hand-clothing stores, the evidence of normal, cheerful lives being lived beside her.

And it worked. She was in Time and Time Again (its wares, as well as its name, were charming), studying a set of dishes that reminded her of some her mother had owned (to be used only when the aunts and uncles came) and feeling a definite respite from anxiety. She toyed with the idea of buying the dishes, looked again, decided they were ugly, really, and wandered over to a jewelry case next to the cash register and the thin young man beside it. It was filled with the usual art nouveau-reproduction pins, a few authentic forties pieces, some cinnebar, things her mother used to call *chotchkes* when she, as a child, had pleaded for them. One piece caught her eye and held it. A small opal brooch, surrounded by seed pearls, sweet and dear.

"May I see that one?" she asked the young man.

He smiled and reached for it. "It's darling, isn't it?"

She returned the smile. (She always admired the way gay men are free to use words without regard to their connotations, for "darling" was surely a woman's word.) "Yes, darling."

She cradled it in her hand and studied the stone, the small red-and-green flashes of light, the tiny graying pearls, and then, turning it over to inspect the clasp, she saw something engraved on it, too small to be read.

"It's got a name on the back," she said to the young man who was still smiling.

"Really?" He held his hand out and she placed the brooch in his palm.

With a magnifying eyepiece he read aloud, " 'To my dear girl.' That's sweet, isn't it?"

"Yes. How much is it?"

"Twenty-five," he said, then, seeing Susan's sour reaction, he added, "but since you're somebody's dear girl, I'll let you have it for eighteen. And you don't even have to have it reengraved."

"How can I resist?" she said, opening her purse.

Later, on the street, she took the brooch out of her purse and admired it again, thinking, I am someone's dear girl, but then she saddened. She doubted whether Lou would describe her in that way. Not now. Not since she had started to upset his days and nights with her hysteria. Not that she hadn't made every attempt to soft-pedal it in front of him; she had, but not with remarkable success. Rather than

shout, she grew sullen. Rather than be grateful for
his help, she resented his misguided attempts at it.

I will not feel sorry for myself, she thought,
remembering Peter and his own shocking news.
(They had not discussed it; they would.)

Up ahead half a block was a small health-food
restaurant and take-out place that Susan had been to
a few times. She recalled their chicken salad Madeira,
a knockout, and decided that, since she had given
herself a present, she would get one for Lou and
Andrea as well. She entered, sniffed the beautiful
odor of homemade mayonnaise and stood in front of
the display case, balancing the chicken salad Madeira
against the shrimps in green sauce.

"Susan? Susan Goodman?"

Susan turned around and saw a woman sitting at a
small table in the corner, waving frantically at her.
The woman's face instantly brought back another
time and place.

"Jennie? Jennie!" And Susan rushed to her.

Jennie Finkelstein (Oh, the name, the horror of
the name, Jennie had always moaned) had gone to
Hunter High School with Susan. They were friends;
dear, funny friends who hadn't seen each other in,
Susan couldn't believe it, twelve years. But Jennie
hadn't been in the States. She had gone into the
foreign service and as far as anyone knew was off in
Kenya or Tibet or someplace equally mythological.

They embraced.

"Oh, my God, look at you! . . ."

"Me? Look at *you!* You look sixteen years old!"

"Double it and then some."

They sat down at the table (or rather crouched
there, straining forward as if to devour each other's

words) and got on to the business of telling each other everything *(everything)* that had happened in the past dozen years.

". . . And then I figured, am I really going to spend my *whole* life without ever having a kosher hot dog? Or reading Li'l Abner or talking without having to interpret every goddamn word," Jennie was saying. "So I put in for a transfer and spent the last two years in Washington, which is, believe me, Bangalore without the flies. But enough about me, tell me what you think of me."

"I think you're wonderful." Susan laughed.

"Of course, what else could a person think? All right, now hit me with the news. You said you're married, what's he like? And you've got a daughter, is she as sensational as her mother? Wait, start at the beginning. When you went to Barnard and I went to Yale—" Jennie raised a pinkie at the mention of Yale —"and we stopped writing, *you* stopped writing."

"I never did. You were so damn busy . . ."

"You ever go to Yale? I had to make a date two weeks in advance to go to the bathroom, just to make sure I'd have time . . ."

Susan ordered a second lunch, completely forgetting the earlier one, and proceeded to tell Jennie her life, moment by moment, or so it seemed. She told her of her first serious affair (Dominic Forte, in whose arms she had lost not only her virginity but for a while, her self respect), of college, disenchantment with her language studies and her parents (oddly, about the same time), her terror of ending up a teacher, her discovery of art as The Way, her near crash when she learned she was not really talented, a summer at Sag Harbor when she met Lou, their courtship, Andrea, everything. Everything except the repulsive thing that called her on the telephone almost daily now. Of that she said nothing, ashamed. (Or was it, she thought fleetingly, that it simply wasn't that important? Not compared to the real issues of her life.)

It was the kind of afternoon that happens, if you're lucky, once in a decade, this chance meeting with someone you truly care for. And when it ground to a halt (Jennie was the first to glance at her watch) Susan was filled with bliss.

But it was a quarter to seven.

They exchanged phone numbers (Jennie was staying at her parents' apartment for another week) and Susan hurried down Columbus Avenue, searching, uselessly, for a cab.

Walking, then almost jogging, she arrived at the apartment, to find Lou and Andrea sitting at the kitchen table, eating scrambled eggs and baked beans.

"Mommy," Andrea said, her mouth a dark-brown smudge. "You're late!"

"Darling, I'm so sorry." Susan kissed Andrea's forehead and looked, almost wincing, at Lou. "I really am."

"Where the hell have you been?"

"Please don't be mad. A thousand apologies. A million subserviences." She tried to wheedle the look of resentment from his face.

"Where were you?" Fear mingled with resentment.

She told him of meeting Jennie but neglected to mention her visit to Peter lest it confirm that fear.

"Couldn't you have called?" His face filled with

weariness. "No, of course you couldn't."

Susan went into the bedroom and stood there in the middle of the room, tasting her aloneness. Then she opened her purse, still in her hand—Lou's attack had come so quickly that she didn't have time to put it down—and withdrew the brooch.

She went back into the kitchen and said to Andrea, "Sweetheart? I have a present for you."

The next attack was that night.

They were sleeping, Susan and Lou (they had said goodnight without ever touching each other), when Sweet William padded into the room, disquieted. He sniffed at the foot of the bed, wanting to come up, but receiving no signal, he went around to Susan's side and stood there, wagging his tail, whining softly. Susan slept. It was not Sweet William's habit to jump on the bed without the signal of permission, but that night, irritated by a force he was helpless to understand, his only hope of sleeping lay in being next to her. He stood up to touch her, but Susan had moved in her sleep to the center of the bed, beyond his reach. He whined but received no response. And so he jumped, awkward (always awkward now that he was old). He hit into the night table on Susan's side and knocked her cigarettes to the floor.

And the phone receiver.

Susan and Lou slept.

She was dreaming; it was a muddle of things past and present. Brian Coleman was there and her father ("Susan, if you hadn't been conceived so early, your brother would have lived"). She was all ages in the dream, entering rooms as a child, leaving them as an adult. Lou was there, too, but he kept leaving her ("I wish I could stay, dear, but you're crazy, you know"). And Sweet William, young and adventurous, whining to run free (her father made her leash him). It was an unpleasant dream, filled with almost forgotten despairs (her mother, furious, crying "What's the use? What's the use?"; Brian's mother telling her he had gone *someplace;* Jennie boarding a bus to India and calling back to Susan, "Have an important life. I will").

And then it darkened.

Brian was the first to fall out of the dream as he had been the first to fall out of her life; he was followed by the others, all of them, father, Lou, Jennie, Andrea, Tara, all of them were gone and Susan was alone. Only Sweet William remained, whining, always whining, gurgling and whining.

There was something else there in the dark. Up ahead of her in the shadows. (But how can there be shadows when everything is blackness?)

Something waiting for her.

In the darker blackness.

She didn't dare move; she tried not to breathe; she wanted to tell Sweet William to stop eating (that was the sound, he was eating) lest the thing in the deeper black know they were there.

"Stop eating, Sweet William! Stop eating now!"

Susan woke.

It was there. Coming from the receiver on the floor. She rolled to the edge of the bed quickly and hung it up.

God, she thought, God, it was here! It was here!

And then she heard the noise, the sound of Sweet William, whining and gurgling and eating. It was coming from across the room. She turned on the light.

Sweet William lay there, in blood, chewing on his paw, looking across the room at his mistress, begging her to make him stop.

7

The next morning, after taking Sweet William to the vet (mercifully, he had done himself minor harm; one toe was chewed to the bone, another merely lacerated), Susan went to the police.

The local precinct, housed in a severe brick building, turn-of-the-century by the look of it, was in itself an effective deterrent to crime. Climbing its stoop of uneven stone steps, even the innocent would chill; the guilty would be consumed with fear.

It was, if anything, worse inside. The quietness of the men (some uniformed, some not) was unnatural, the barrenness of the furnishings disconcerting, the very walls (white but in need of painting) were cold and offensive.

On a bench, to one side of the entry room, a black boy sat, his eyes red, a parent on either side of him, muttering obscenities.

Susan, frightened, approached the long desk facing the boy and tried to explain what had brought her there. She was speaking to a uniformed policeman who looked at her directly, bleakly, uncaringly.

She was told to sit on the bench, near the boy.

Policemen came in and went out as she sat there; some she could envision as saviors, others looked more brutal than those they hunted.

And her feelings of guilt mounted.

After ten painful minutes, Susan was shown past the desk, through a door into a large communal room filled with desks and policemen. People were being interviewed (interrogated?) at these desks, and most looked to her dangerous. She wished she hadn't come there, to the center of a system that deals daily with horror and viciousness (the bowels of the city, like its sewers, reek).

The man she spoke to was called Kevin Mulay. No other designation was announced (Sergeant, Captain, Detective). He was, happily, polite to her and didn't stare so much as look intently at her, trying to sort out what she was saying (rambling, accusing).

But even to Susan it sounded insane.

To his credit, Kevin Mulay never openly expressed his certainty that he was dealing with a sick woman, but it was apparent all the same. He explained to her that unless a crime had been committed there was nothing the police could do. He assured her (to her dismay) that they had not received comparable complaints. As to the question of the dog's self-induced attack, he could only shrug. And with that shrug, he stood up, offered her his hand, and dismissed her.

Outside (once again in the natural world) Susan felt a mixture of relief and hopelessness.

She spent the afternoon at the office bickering with

Tara ("Jesus, Susan, you're letting this thing get to you. Yuri says . . .") and color-correcting proofs of one of her illustrations (Cool Cucumber Days and What to Do with Them). But this time she found no relief in work, no respite from the image of Sweet William cowering in the dark of her bedroom, frightened and frightening.

As to Lou, they had spoken briefly when she woke him (he bandaged Sweet William) but it was the middle of the night and they compromised on spending the next evening alone together (Andrea would stay with her grandmother) to discuss it. Susan anticipated that meeting with much the same despair with which she answered any ringing phone (if she indeed answered it).

And so a despondent afternoon led to an unavoidable evening.

She arrived home to find Andrea watching television, flanked by two hostile elderly women, one, the usurped, Mrs. Diamond, the other, the usurper, Susan's mother.

"She lets Andrea watch television every afternoon?" her mother complained after Mrs. Diamond had quietly stormed out of the apartment.

"What else should she do, Mom? She's tired after school—" and too late Susan remembered the best way to shut her mother up was to agree with her.

"I never let you watch television, not when there were better things to do."

"Right, you're right."

"A child's mind needs stimulation. When you came home from school, I used to sit with you and draw pictures. That's why you're an artist today."

In what dream did you sit with me? "You're right" came out.

"That was always our time together, when you came home from school, before Poppa got home. . . ."

That was your time with the chickens, Mom. "I remember."

"And then he'd come in and look at your pictures and make a fuss. . . ." The old woman's eyes stared off into the past of her making, and Susan, seeing it, put her arm around her and lied, "It was good, Mom."

"Yes, it was. You remember Mrs. Franklin?"

"No."

"Of course you remember Mrs. Franklin. . . ."

"If I remember her, why did you ask me?"

"She lived downstairs in Three B. She gave you her old records. . . ."

"Oh, yeah, I remember," Susan said because it was easier.

"She used to ask for your pictures. She hung some in her kitchen, now you remember?"

"I said I remember." And Susan went into the kitchen, hoping her mother would take the hint and leave.

"Don't let her watch television after school." The old woman followed relentlessly. "Get her a little watercoloring set, like I got you. . . ."

In the dear dead days beyond recall. "Good idea."

"Being a good mother takes thinking ahead." Susan leaned against the sink and looked to heaven for patience.

"Andrea, get your things. Grammy's waiting," she called out.

Within five minutes Andrea and her grandmother were out the door, but not before the latter had dispensed a few more words of wisdom. "It wouldn't hurt you to take her to the office when there's no school, so she sees that women also work. . . ." "You want Andrea to do something? Praise her. It does no good to blame. . . ." "You look tired. What time do you go to bed? . . ."

Alone, Susan sat in the living room and smoked a cigarette.

One down. One to go.

At six-thirty, that one arrived home, his distaste for what lay ahead obvious. Susan wisely chose not to broach the subject until after dinner, and as she cooked (*steak au poivre,* a bribe for Lou to be supportive) she tried not to notice Sweet William hobbling around, biting at his bandage.

After a desultory dinner in which Susan's mood altered ("What am I feeling guilty for? What have I done?") Lou started.

"Honey, I've been thinking—" and the words tiptoed out of him as if landing on eggs. "I can swing a week off now. If you'd like, we could get your mother to stay with Andrea. . . ."

It was the wrong tack.

Susan got up quickly from the table, nearly upsetting her chair.

"I'm not crazy, Lou. I'm not inventing these things." She went quickly into the living room and lit a cigarette.

"I didn't mean it that way," he said, following.

"No? How did you mean it, Lou? Why should we go away? You think it won't reach me wherever we go?'' It was beginning to occur to her how angry she was with him; how resentful of his guilt-inducing *tolerance*.

''Honey, calm down. . . .''

''*You* be calm. Nothing's happening to *you!*'' And she ground the cigarette out on a silver ashtray they never used. ''Except maybe your precious serenity is being upset. But I can't be calm! I'm the one scared shitless!''

He tried to hold her but she would have none of it; no more condescension, no more *generosity*.

''I don't know what to do for you, Susan,'' he said, and the honesty of it moved her.

''You don't have to do anything for me.'' She allowed him to take her hands in his. ''Just live through it with me. Don't turn me into some kind of fool, okay?''

''I'm sorry. I just don't understand any of it.''

''Well, join the club.''

''I want to, Susan, believe me—'' and she did. ''But it isn't easy. You answer the phone, there's no one there. . . .''

''There *is* someone there. Why can't I make you understand that? There *is* someone there!''

She walked away from him and looked out the window. She could see a family having dinner across the street in one of the apartments. One of them was actually laughing. (Thank God someone was still laughing.)

''Look—'' and she turned back to him, once again guilty (against her will). ''Let me try to explain it to you as it happened. . . .''

Lou listened, not interrupting, for nearly ten minutes, and in that time he took Susan's hand and held it, stroking it self-consciously.

This time she told him everything: Yuri, her visit to Peter and the police.

By the look on his face, Susan knew she was frightening Lou.

"I had no idea it had gone that far," he said.

"Well, it has."

They were silent for a moment, reconnoitering, and then Lou said gently, "Are you going to see that doctor?"

"Yes." And she could have guessed his reaction. The lawyer had weighed the evidence and come up with his verdict.

Innocent by virtue of insanity.

The specialist Peter sent her to was surprisingly young—barely Susan's age, but in those few professional years he had already adopted an air of unquestioning superiority. As she told him about the calls, watching carefully to see some flash of incredulity amid the smugness, he merely listened and nodded as if he were hearing symptoms of a common cold.

And then the tests started.

Balance, eyes, ears, taste (sour or sweet, bitter, bland?), touch (warm, cool, rough, smooth?); color sense (which blue is most like this one?); smell (flowers, soap, perfume?).

And the questions. (Any headaches, backaches, tiredness, flashes of color, irregularity of menstrual cycle, soreness, weakness in fingers and toes, sleeplessness, nightmares, bed-wetting?)

A dozen machines clicked at her; reams of paper were used up.

And then, when the examination was over, he smiled for the first time (who would have thought it? A sweet smile) and let her go (remembering, almost as an afterthought, that she should see his nurse, who would take a blood and a urine sample).

Thus, humiliated once more, Susan hailed a cab and spent the rest of the afternoon (another day of work missed) in bed, vacantly watching television.

8

The time for warning had come.

Susan had spent a loathsome afternoon at the office (Maudey had dropped in on her no less than three times to complain, solicitously, of her frequent absences: "But, sweetie, what on earth is going on? You've always been one of my *stalwarts!*"). Tara was no help ("Listen, hon, just between us, is something up between you and Lou? That kind of thing can make anything seem worse than it is. . . ."); and work was impossible (how many times can you sketch a bowl of peaches that consistently come out yellow apples?). And so at four-thirty Susan left the office, guiltily looking around for Maudey, and made her way to the subway.

The uptown Broadway train was its usual bizarre self, the faces staring ahead, not wanting to look at you lest you take it as an insult, the straphangers wobbling back and forth for a secure position, the

loud black and white and tan teenagers having fun as
if it were a duty. And, of course, the obligatory weird
one, sitting off alone, lecturing the air.

And then the train stopped at Sixty-sixth Street
and waited, doors closed.

Susan, sitting (a blessing) and facing the platform,
watched the people standing at the door waiting to
get in. A few of them looked confused (the train is in,
why aren't the doors opening?), a few annoyed, but
most just dead, like the ones already in the train, in
transit emotionally as well as literally.

She glanced around the platform, at the bill-
boards (shows, girdles, cigarettes), at the evidence
that "Juan of 136th Street" was still alive and well,
to the booth where two middle-aged black women in
sweaters dispensed the tokens, to the door of the
men's room from which an elderly man emerged
still zipping up his fly, to the row of phones on the
wall . . .

One of which was dripping.

Susan looked around a man who had just taken the
strap over her head to see it more clearly.

One phone among three. Dripping.

Rivulets moving down the tile wall behind it to the
floor.

Red rivulets.

The color of Sweet William's paw.

She did nothing.

And then the train pulled out, never opening its
doors, leaving those inside wanting to get out, those
outside wanting to get in, and Susan, staring, doing
nothing.

Blood. And then locusts.

It was the next day, and Susan, having slept a total

of three hours the night before, exhausted, confused, despairing, chose not to go to work. (What Maudey would think never even occurred to her.) Lou and Andrea gone, she wandered through the rooms of the apartment, made countless cups of tea (a learned response to feeling ill) and tried not to think.

But thoughts, nonetheless, were circling, joining together into theories and descending, hawklike, on her.

The maiming of animals (Sweet William, the squirrel).

The unexplainable things (the taxi driver with Brian Coleman's name, the bleeding phone).

The Silence itself, which sought her out at the theater, the restaurant, anywhere.

Somewhere lay a meaning to all of it, an explanation she could tell Lou and Peter and the police—if only she could find it.

"Sweet William, what are you doing?" She heard him scratching at something in the living room. "Stop it."

She was in the kitchen now, preparing another cup of tea, remembering how it was when she was little and sick and her mother would cater to her (as if she'd just discovered she had a daughter). There was a watercoloring set (her mother was right, after all) but it had only arrived after two days of the flu. And there was a set of Classic Comics (the measles?).

"Quit it!"

Andrea had worn the opal brooch to school that morning. Susan congratulated herself. The sins of the mother will not be passed on to the daughter.

"What is with you?" She turned off the stove—she didn't really want another cup of tea—and went into the living room.

Sweet William was lying on his side under a table, scratching at the wall.

"Stop it, nut." The dog ignored her. "Come on, S.W. . . ." Susan took him by the hind legs and pulled him out from under the table. "You hide a bone under there?"

He looked up at her, ashamed, drew his ears back and, in his characteristic and incredibly sweet way, pushed his face forward to be kissed. Susan sat cross-legged on the floor and took the large old dog in her arms, forcing him backward into her lap so that his hind legs stood up in the air.

"You're just a baby," she said, kissing him. "You're just Mommy's crazy baby."

He turned his face around and in one swipe drenched her cheek.

"Yuch," she said, releasing him. "Go brush your teeth."

Taking it as an admonishment, he flattened his ears again and pushed forward to be kissed, knocking Susan over on her side.

"Get away from me, you smelly thing," she said, laughing, and he pushed into her, tail going as well as wet, odorous tongue.

Thus, temporarily rallied by the aptly named dog, Susan dressed and went marketing, her mind distracted. The price of groceries further distracted her (being, if not as disastrous as the Silence, at least on the same continuum), and as she left the supermarket, she felt somewhat repaired.

Homeostasis. The word came back to her in the elevator. Peter had explained it to her years before. Homeostasis. The body fighting to return to normal, to its balanced state. The mind must be homeostatic, oo, she thought, counting what appeared to be her only blessing at that moment.

Sweet William met her at the door as he always did, hoping that something in the bag of groceries was for him. Together they went into the kitchen, and Susan started to unpack.

Out of the corner of her eye, she saw it.

It was under the table, crawling.

Without so much as a shudder, she ripped off a length of paper toweling from the overhead rack and went to scoop up the roach (she was, after all, raised in New York).

It was a grasshopper.

She looked at it questioningly. A grasshopper in early spring on the eleventh floor of an apartment house on West End Avenue? With that, she brought the toweling down over it, balled it and tossed it in the trash pail.

Then she saw another, near the sink.

"What?" she said aloud, seeing a third crawl in from the hall.

And a fourth.

Had they been roaches, she would have felt a familiar revulsion, but grasshoppers reminded her of summer camp and Riverside Park, hardly creatures to be afraid of.

And a fifth entered from the hall.

Perplexed, Susan stepped over it (still unafraid) and went into the hall.

There were dozens there, streaming out from the living room.

Now she was frightened.

She crossed over them (jumping; crushing one) and looked in the living room.

Hundreds.

All crawling out from under the table where Sweet William had been scratching earlier. An army of grasshoppers, crawling and hopping into her home. She could hear them now—the clicking of their legs.

She hurried back into the kitchen (jumping from space to space, nonetheless crushing some) and got a broom. Then, sweeping her way to the living-room table, she looked under it.

Sweet William had dislodged a small metal box that was attached to the wall. From the box an electrical cord led to . . .

The phone.

And from the hole behind the box, now uncovered, came the grasshoppers. As Susan watched they fought their way out, another dozen, green, chirping, mandibles clicking, spindly awkward legs pulling them out.

"Oh, Christ!" she screamed. "Christ!"

She grabbed the first thing she saw (a clock on the table), pushed the box back over the hole, lodged the clock in front of it. She had cut one of the grasshoppers in half; its head hung out, bodyless, from behind the box.

She got up quickly, fearing they would get on her and fled the apartment.

Outside in the hall, breathless, stunned, shaking, she rang for the elevator and took it to the basement. Tito, the handyman, a round-faced good-natured Cuban, was hauling trash.

"Morning, Mrs.," he said, never sure of any of the tenants' names. "Nice day, huh?"

"Tito, I need your help!"

It was not the first time he'd seen a Mrs. in that

tate of anxiety; usually it was brought on by a leak
or a blown fuse just before company was due. Once
an elderly Mrs. fetched him in tears over nothing
more serious than a stopped-up pilot light. Tito had
seen it all.

But he had never seen this before.

Susan led him to the apartment and, refusing to
enter herself, waited in the hall while he cleaned them
up. Then, leaving with a plastic garbage bag full of
them, he said, "You can go in now, Mrs., I think I
got 'em all." He avoided asking where the grasshoppers had come from. It did no good to ask too many
questions: tenants liked their privacy. (She probably
brought them in herself. Why? Rich North Ameri-
cans are crazy, that's why.)

Tentatively Susan entered the apartment. Sweet
William, the cause of it all, was sleeping. Slowly she
made herself a cup of tea, and even more slowly she
understood.

"Enough already, Susan, *Please,*" Lou said, later
in the evening, when Susan told him.

"Please, Lou, don't fight with me. . . ."

"Susan, listen to what you're saying!"

"I know what I'm saying. . . ." And she tried to be
quiet so that Andrea wouldn't hear them from her
room.

"Christ," Lou muttered, pacing the kitchen, fully
aware that his wife was in the midst of a breakdown,
a breakdown they would all pay for.

"It's in the Bible," she said for the hundredth
time.

"Don't give me that crap about the Bible!" Then,
softening, he went to her. "Honey, you don't really
believe any of this, do you?"

She had wanted to cry for days, and now, finally, she permitted it.

"Honey, don't . . ."

"I'm not crazy, Lou . . ."

"Nobody said you were, but . . ."

"It's in the Bible." And she buried her face in his chest, sobbing.

He held her, felt the wave of sympathy and love for her, which gave way too quickly to thoughts of doctors (hospitals?), treatment, taking care of Andrea on his own, the whole dreadful litany of a home broken apart by illness.

"I can prove it," she said suddenly, pushing away from him, going to the back door.

"Honey, don't . . ." But before she could hear him, Susan was out the door. She rang for the service elevator as Lou followed her out of the apartment.

"Come inside."

"No, I want to prove it."

"Susan, please, we can deal with it ourselves" (without the building's staff telling the other tenants).

"No."

"Please . . ."

"No!"

The service elevator screeched into motion and in a moment, the door was opened by a gray-haired man.

"Abe," Susan said, "is Tito still here?"

"No, Mrs. Reed. Tito's gone. Is there anything I can do?"

"Is he on tomorrow?"

"Tito? Didn't you hear?"

"Hear what?" And she saw, in her mind, Tito destroyed so that he couldn't help her. Destroyed, struck down, *smote*.

"Tito retired. Today was his last day. I thought everybody knew."

They went back into the apartment, Susan, grateful that Tito hadn't been harmed (he could have been, now she knew that), Lou, almost sick with worry himself.

And the phone rang.

"Don't answer it," Susan said.

"Honey . . ."

"Don't answer it!"

He did. It was Susan's mother. He held the phone out to her and at first she refused it, but then, knowing she had to win him over, she did as he asked her.

"Hello." And she tried not to listen, not to hear what might be on the other end of the line (now that she alone could hear it).

"Susan?" It was as Lou said, her mother's voice. "I have bad news."

"What?" and though she asked, she had a sickening feeling she already knew.

"It's Jimmy," the older woman went on, herself crying. "It's Jimmy."

Susan listened, numb, and when her mother had finished, she said, "Take something, Momma. Take something and lie down. I'll come over," and she hung up.

Seeing her face, ashen, in shock, Lou asked, "What?"

"My cousin," she said, almost without emotion. "He was in a car accident."

"Jesus, honey . . ." He started toward her.

"And the firstborn will die."

"What?"

She looked up at him. How could he still not understand? But it didn't matter. Nothing mattered. Her body was pumped full of glandular secretions which, added to the lack of sleep, prevented any further stress.

"It's in the Bible," she said. "The plagues Moses brought against Egypt." And she yearned for sleep.

9

Peter smiled across at her, a wistful smile, but beneath it was the same look she had seen earlier on Lou's face—the melancholy acceptance of the fact that she was sick.

For a moment she tried to imagine that they were right, but that was useless, for they weren't.

"You never believed in God," Peter said.

It was true enough; she had always held that she was an atheist, never accepting the label "agnostic" as most of her friends did; that had always seemed a compromise to her.

"I was never damned before," she said.

Peter paused, considering how best to answer her. "Do you feel you deserve to be damned?"

It was funny to hear him use the same tactics for this that he had used, years before, to wipe away her petty guilts and fears.

"I don't know."

"What have you done?"

"Nothing." And in the time it took to say it she remembered a nameless brother whom she had killed (somehow that was the message her mother had instilled in her) and the death of a father that had hardly affected her.

"Then why would you deserve to be damned?" Peter went on in his gentle, logical way.

"I don't know, Peter. Somebody's got to do it." She smiled ruefully.

"Is the possibility of coincidence completely out of the question?" he then asked.

"Yes, completely."

"Is there a possibility that someone is doing all of this to you? Someone who . . ."

"Peter," she interrupted, "you know there are only two possibilities. Either God is punishing me or I'm crazy."

He didn't answer.

"You know that's the truth, don't you?"

"Yes," he finally admitted.

"And you've already cast your ballot." He avoided her eyes. "It isn't God to you, is it?"

"No, but it isn't *crazy* either." And she recalled how he loathed that word. "The body is an incredible mechanism. One gland the size of a dime goes off schedule and like dominoes all systems back up and go haywire. Anything can happen. . . ."

"But you had me checked out. There's nothing wrong with me."

"Susan, we only scratched the surface. There's nothing *obviously* wrong with you, but who knows? You're a smart, well-adjusted woman. Hallucinations like these mean something's gone wrong, something we haven't traced yet. . . ."

She envied him his certainty that they were hallucinations.

"You don't believe in God, do you, Peter?"

"No, not at all," he answered without hesitation.

"Listen, maybe *you're* crazy. Two hundred
million Frenchmen can't be wrong.

"Can and are and I think you know it. Susan—"
he took her hand—"you're not a woman prone to
this kind of nervous disorder. You're a normal person, a strong one. If you react in this outrageous a
way, I'd be willing to bet money it's not emotional,
it's physical. Something's fucked up."

In the two years that she'd seen him, Peter had
never cursed. It looked oddly sweet on him—as if he
were affronted by her problems.

"Trust me, Peter," she said. "It's real. It isn't extrasensory garbage or mid-life crisis or some gland
gone berserk. Every bit of it is real."

"Or seems it," he insisted.

They argued (affectionately) for the rest of her
session, and then Susan, still touched by his concern,
kissed Peter's cheek and left, promising to be back
the following day.

But before her next session with Peter, there was
another torture she had to endure.

Jimmy's funeral.

At eleven o'clock the next morning, Susan and
Lou and her mother entered Riverside Chapel, took
the elevator to the third floor and met the rest of the
family.

The first one she saw was Ida, Jimmy's mother,
sitting across the room, stunned and red-faced. She
was nodding slowly to those who tried to comfort
her; someone was crying, not she. On her face were a

thousand years of Jewish torment, all the suffering and the prayers and the courage were there, those at Dachau were there in her eyes, the starving hordes from played-out farms in Poland, those who had been put to death in the Middle Ages, all there, looking out of her eyes, not asking "Why me?" but knowing why, hating it, accepting it.

The coffin lay in the corner of the room, behind a turn in the wall, so that those who wanted to see it could and the rest would be spared.

They were talking to someone, another cousin Susan remembered, a second cousin. Susan said little, afraid that if she spoke too much she'd tell them all that Jimmy died, not because of anything he had done, but because of her.

As part of her damnation.

The blood, the locusts, the death of the firstborn.

"Come to Ida with me," her mother, already crying, said.

Susan obeyed but said nothing when Ida took her in her arms (as much to avoid her sister's tears as to embrace her niece) but then, when Ida asked, "How's Andrea?" Susan found herself weeping and repeating over and over, "I'm so sorry."

Shortly after, they were shown downstairs to a small reception room next to the chapel. Susan's grief (guilt) mingled with the blameless tears of others, and no one thought anything of the cousin who seemed so deeply affected by the tragedy.

Several hours later, still in her dark-blue funeral dress, Susan arrived at Peter's office.

"Susan," he said after they had discussed the funeral and she had gotten the crying out of the way, "I want you to do something for me. I know it sounds far out, but I want you to do it anyway."

"What?" she was surprised to see how insistent he was.

"Have I ever mentioned my brother to you?"

"Jack the genius?" He had indeed mentioned him, many times, to show his own insecurity ("It's a natural function of being human to be insecure," he had said), as well as his feelings of jealousy and rivalry (also natural, normal).

"I had dinner with him last night and he was doing his usual bragging . . ."

"Did you do your usual resenting?"

"Not this time. I think Jack may be able to help you. . . ."

"Aha, I forgot. Jack's a doctor, too."

"*The* doctor. I'm the black sheep of the family, he's the messiah—" and Peter allowed some resentment out in retrospect. "He's one of the researchers in charge of a pretty large facility on Long Island. They're working with a new device, a brain scanner. Jack thinks it's going to revolutionize psychiatric evaluation. Anyway, what it does, simply, is to take pictures of the activity of the brain, to tell whether it's functioning normally or not. . . ."

"Like an X ray?"

"No. An X ray can only show you the structures, not what's going on with them. Look, what happens is this, they inject a glucose-like substance into you . . ."

"Into *me?*"

He hesitated. "I hope so, if you'll permit it. Let me tell you, I had to stand on my head and spit nickels to get Jack to consider doing a brain scan on you. They're not like free chest X rays. But he does need subjects and . . ."

"And I'm a likely candidate for brain disease," Susan added, smiling quickly to show that it was a joke (it wasn't).

"And if something's wrong, this machine can spot it, if Jack isn't full of shit, which, believe me, he never is."

"How does it work?" Susan asked, meaning "Will it hurt?"

"It's so beautifully simple—" Peter was excited, despite the sibling rivalry. "Basically, what they inject is food, to be used by the brain in its normal metabolism, and then, while the brain is *eating* the stuff, they photograph cross sections of it. What they end up with is a series of computer pictures showing where the sugar is being consumed. And here's the incredible part" (again the excitement). "There's a difference in the consumption of sugar in various parts of the brain due to physical or emotional problems. You can actually *see* it!"

"How do you photograph a cross section of the brain?" Susan pictured needle-sized scalpels being driven into her head.

"The glucose is radioactively tagged." He saw the fear in her eyes. "Look, it's an incredibly low level of radioactivity. There's nothing to be afraid of, unless you can't take the shot in the arm."

"And what if it doesn't find anything wrong?" Susan asked.

"What if it does?"

She agreed to think it over and let Peter know.

Susan went to a synagogue.

She hadn't been to one in years, and sitting there alone, looking at the artifacts of her childhood, she was overwhelmed with a sense of loss and regret. (I that why she'd been damned, because of her turning away from God?)

One stained-glass window depicted the Passover seder, a meal she hadn't had in . . . decades. (Was that the reason?) Another, Moses leading the people of Israel out of Egypt (the blood, the locusts, the death of the firstborn).

There was a prayer book on the back of the bench in front of her. She lifted it from its rack and thumbed through it, looking at the bewildering Hebrew words, the arch English translations (. . . and blessed be the lighter of candles . . .).

She remembered the high holy days when her father was alive and she and her mother sat upstairs in the temple while he (privileged) sat downstairs with the men, and the day her mother told her that he had a disease (she never said "cancer" though cancer it was), and the funeral at which she'd been bored and thought about the food waiting for them at the apartment.

She remembered Brian Coleman's death and the book of his she'd kept instead of sending it back to his parents and the times she had masturbated and the lies she had told. She remembered the men she had slept with whom she didn't love (or even like, particularly) and the times she'd been short-tempered with Andrea and unfair (perhaps even cruel) and the awful things she'd wished on people she hated and her private satisfaction when some of them happened.

And she decided.

She had done nothing to bring this horror upon herself. If God had damned her, it was an evil God who had chosen her at random.

She was innocent.

*   *   *

Three mornings later, Lou went to Olin's to pick up the car he had rented to drive Susan to Jack Steinman's laboratory.

And the thing called.

Susan, now knowing how not to listen to it, shouted to it, "I haven't done anything!" and she imagined her words sucked into its void. "Leave me alone! I haven't done anything!"

She hung up and, remarkably unshaken for an encounter with it, went downstairs to wait for Lou.

"Honey?" Lou said as Susan watched the ugly highways go by.

"What?"

"I'm sorry."

"For what?"

"You know what for."

She did, indeed. "It's all right," she said, only half lying, and went back to staring at the flat, dreary outline of Long Island.

Jack Steinman looked so much like Peter that Susan trusted him immediately. He met them in the main hall of the building, which resembled a college library more than a medical installation, and took them upstairs to a small waiting room where he left them briefly. He had been friendly enough, but non-talkative. He said the test would take two hours, during which Lou might like to have lunch in the cafeteria (he warned him about the food, his sole attempt at charm). And when he returned (they had waited silently, Lou pacing, Susan sitting quite still, quite frightened), two other members of the staff were with him; a Dr. Jane Meternick (fifties, overweight, pretty) and a younger man, a Mr. Fox. Dr. Meternick assured Susan there was nothing to be concerned about (Susan's face was, by now, a mask of anxiety), and she was led off, leaving Lou standing with Mr. Fox, presumably receiving some words of comfort himself.

It was nothing like Susan had imagined.

She was not, for example, required to disrobe or wear a white gown (she was sure she would be). The testing room looked more like a stereo warehouse to her than a laboratory; machines everywhere, filing cabinets, amplifiers, desks, a clutter. A clutter of people as well—she counted twelve—all going about their business, paying her no attention (she assumed they had been told to do so, so as not to embarrass her).

She was required to lie down on a stretcher, the end of which was attached to the room's largest machine and the only one that seemed malevolent. For the end of the stretcher was pushed up against a circular opening in the machine, and in that opening she could see blazing lights, like an oven.

"There's absolutely no discomfort," Dr. Meternick said. "The lights are a little warm, that's all. Pretend you're in Miami, lolling around the Fontainebleau."

"I've never been in Miami," Susan said, aware that Dr. Meternick was rubbing the inside of her arm with an alcohol swab.

"Me either." She produced a hypodermic syringe from a nearby table. "I once got as far as Birmingham, Alabama, though. That turned me off the South. I'm going to inject you now. Please hold your arm still, it'll only take a second. . . ." The needle stung but no more than a hundred needles Susan had had before. "I was visiting my husband's family. My *ex*-husband, thank God."

Susan waited for some change in the way she felt, some reaction to the drug that now was inside her, but none came. Her breathing was shallow, as it had been, from fear; she still felt slightly dizzy, the same cause.

"We'll wait a little while," Dr. Meternick continued, "before we start the scan. So, you have children, Mrs. Reed?"

"Susan. Yes, I have a daughter."

"How old?"

"Eight."

"That's a wonderful age. My daughter is nineteen. That's not a wonderful age. All I get from her is how old-fashioned I am, how stupid I am. . . ."

"How could she think you stupid?" Susan was grateful for the woman's humanness. "Look at what you do for a living."

"Research? *Feh*. Research is for idiots, haven't you heard?"

"*Poor* idiots," a male voice from the other side of the room added.

"Tell me about it," the doctor continued. "My daughter has fourteen pair of shoes. I have five. What can one human being do with fourteen pair of shoes?"

"Walk all over her mother," the male voice answered.

"You have to pardon him," the doctor said to Susan. "He's met my daughter."

"What does she want to be?" Susan asked, feeling better, more secure, glad that this room was still part of the real world where mothers and daughters fought.

"God help me, a model. I ask you, is that a fitting punishment for a woman who's got three degrees, that her daughter wants to be a model? Okay, Susan—" and the tone of her voice altered, growing deeper, more in charge—"now I'd like you to move up on the bed and rest your head inside the opening." She helped her, hand under Susan's head, until Susan could feel the soft foam-rubber padding beneath her neck. Her head inside the giant machine, her eyes closed against the glare of the lights, her heart pumping quickly now.

"So you're in Miami with the other rich ladies trying to decide which new dress to buy, that's right, keep your eyes closed, there's nothing to see anyway, and you look in a magazine, say *Vogue,* and there's this pretty nineteen-year-old in just the perfect dress. The dress is yours, the nineteen-year-old is mine. . . ." And Susan heard a short high-pitched buzz, a zap, go off next to her. ". . . Don't tense up, that's just the sound of the scanner . . . it's nothing. . . . Do you have any other children, Susan?"

"No."

"I do. I have a son. Twenty-four. He's a resident at Mount Sinai. An internist . . ."

"Two Doctor Meternicks," Susan muttered, trying not to hear the zaps that were coming every few seconds now.

"Only that's not his name. I use my maiden name. After all those years of study, why should I give his family the credit?"

"What does he do, your ex-husband?" Susan asked.

Zap.

"Besides aggravate me? He manufactures useless objects. Woman's hats . . ."

Zap.

". . . So Gloria takes after him and Neal takes after me. . . ."

Zap.

". . . I guess the world needs hats as well as truth. . . ."

Zap.

"Why don't you doze off for a while, Susan? There's nothing you have to do and it can't be much fun listening to my complaining. . . ."

After a while, Susan did doze off, never falling truly asleep but lulled into peace by the warmth on her face and the soft, sweet, funny voice of Dr. Meternick.

10

Susan had the phones removed.

It was several days after Peter told her the brain scan had revealed nothing (his disappointment, instead of touching her, made her irritable. "*Now* will you believe me?").

After an argument with Tara: ("Susan, it's all you talk about!" "What else am I supposed to talk about? What's new at Bloomingdale's? Jesus, Tara, what's the matter with you?").

And Maudey: ("Look, I'm sorry for taking so much time off but there's nothing I can do about it. If you can't wait until this thing is over, I'll understand your replacing me . . .").

And her mother: ("Nothing is the matter. Will you just leave me alone?").

She decided one morning that it was her home, that no one (no thing, no power, no deity however malignant) had the right to offend her in her own

93

home. And so she called the phone company (Tara dialed as if she were doing her the most monumental favor in the world) and arranged to have the phones removed (ripped out, shredded for all she cared).

And then Lou found out.

She was in the kitchen preparing dinner (resenting it; resenting everything for days) when Lou, who had come home and played with Andrea without noticing the three barren spots, one beside their bed, one in the living room, one beside her in the kitchen, entered, still unaware.

"What's for dinner?" he asked innocently.

"Chops." She volunteered no further information, knowing that soon enough they would be fighting. (Where to send Andrea? She'd surely hear them in her room.)

"Lamb, veal, mutton, what?"

"Pork."

"Don't be silly. It's not in your heritage to make pork chops." He lifted the lid on the skillet. "Lamb," he announced, as if she didn't know.

It suddenly, and for no apparent reason, occurred to Susan that they hadn't made love in days (weeks?).

"Give a holler when it's ready." Lou left the room.

"I'll holler, all right," she said under her breath, now looking forward to it.

They ate, and he still didn't notice.

Then, with Andrea ensconced in front of the nightly lunacy on TV, Lou called to her from the bedroom.

She joined him, closing the door after her. He was standing by the night table, looking at it, not in any of the attitudes she'd expected—neither exhausted patience nor condescending understanding. He was angry.

They fought, as she had wanted. ("Susan, I can't live in a home without a telephone. It's insane!" "It's my home, too, and I'm not having that *thing* call me here!")

They tended Andrea. ("We're just having a little argument, honey. Nothing to be upset over. Go watch 'Three's Company'. . . .")

They calmed down. ("But how can we live like this? Susan, suppose someone has to reach us?" "They can call next door. That's what my parents did before they had a phone. . . .")

And finally they compromised. Lou would have another phone installed, for his use only. Susan was not to be expected to answer it if it rang; Lou would take all calls.

"How long is it going to be like this?" Lou asked, drained of all his anger (and sympathy?).

"Until it's over."

"Will you continue seeing Peter?"

"Yes." (For all the good it will do.)

He made an attempt at holding her, failed (she broke away first, sensing he was about to) and joined Andrea, who was by now sullen at having been left out of the argument, in front of the TV set.

Susan, sitting on the bed, having won the battle despite the phone he would order (it wasn't her phone nor her responsibility), decided to leave the apartment.

"I'm going for a walk," she told Lou, who was beyond disagreeing with her about anything. (You don't argue with crazy people, she thought, riding down in the elevator.)

Outside, it was cool and quiet; no arguments, no strained understanding, no unspoken blame. She turned north and walked up West End Avenue, past the doormen and the canopied buildings, now seedier than they were when she was a child and only the rich lived in them, past the schools (John-John Kennedy had gone to Collegiate, diagonally across from their building, a source of West Side pride), across Eighty-sixth Street (she had had no less than three friends who lived on Eighty-sixth, between West End and the Drive), into the low Nineties where the side streets spilled garbage to announce the welfare hotels. And then, at Ninety-third, she found herself looking up at one of the apartment houses, remembering the many times she'd entered its marble lobby, school briefcase pulling her to a slant.

It was Jennie Finkelstein's building.

Jennie, who was here, in New York. Jennie, whose sympathy she had not yet drained.

Susan hurried into the building but was stopped by the locked interior doors (the first sign of deterioration—no doorman). She went to the row of tenant names and mercifully found it, Finkelstein, 6R, pressed its intercom button and waited by the mouthpiece.

Please be here, Jennie. Please!

"Hello? Yes?" A woman's voice, metallic, called down to her.

"Mrs. Finkelstein?" Susan shouted into the mouthpiece. "Is Jennie there?" *("Can she come out and play? It's Susie.")*

"Jennie? Who is this?"

"It's Susan Goodman, a friend of hers from Hunter High. . . ."

"Oh, my God, Susie? Is that you?"

"Yes. I met Jennie the other day. She said she was staying with you. . . ."

"Wait, darling. Come upstairs. Nat, it's Susie Goodman downstairs . . ." and the buzzer went off, clicking the doors open.

She pushed through them into the lobby and felt sickened by what she saw. The walls dirty, paint peeling (painted marble, not real as she had always assumed), the wooden mantel over the fake fireplace marred with initials, the carpet, once wine-colored and elegant, now frayed and filthy. It was like meeting an old friend, once robust, who had been stricken and was now wasted away, giving only hints at what had once been. Stepping into the elevator, she again saw the scratched graffiti *(Hector sucks)* and felt a wave of resentment and anger. Who were these people who took it on themselves to destroy her memories? Were their names, sprayed or cut, their only proof of being? If so . . . before she could complete the awful thought, the elevator door opened and Susan saw Mrs. Finkelstein standing behind her door, peering out expectantly.

"My God, look at you!" she said. (Weren't those Jennie's words, too?) "What a sight for sore eyes!" (Those, surely, were not.)

She was escorted in, a princess from the past, and forced to have coffee with the aging couple. (Her mother had fared better than Jennie's, Susan saw, for the woman was stooped, arthritic and worry-worn. Nat Finkelstein also looked old, thin, badgered.)

"No, darling, Jennie went back to Washington over a week ago," the mother was saying as they settled down in the living room.

Susan looked around at the furnishings. Had

everyone of that generation bought the same things, had the same taste (lack of it)?

"So, what'd you think of our politician?" the father asked proudly.

"She's wonderful, just wonderful."

"And you, sweetheart?" The mother poured coffee. "Are you married?"

Right to the point. "Yes."

"Children?"

Susan felt she should lie out of loyalty to Jennie, but she didn't. "Yes, a daughter."

"A daughter." The father smiled. "A daughter." And it occurred to Susan that this couple, aging badly and living in remnants of their former life, had one source of unabused happiness left—their daughter.

"You must be so proud of Jennie," she said kindly. "One of these days we're going to be hearing about *Senator* Finkelstein."

"If only it were a different name," the mother said, and for a moment Susan thought she, like her daughter, was poking fun at it. Then she realized it was a maiden name.

"She's still young," Susan said.

"She's thirty-seven. When I was thirty-seven, she was already in school. . . ."

"Don't complain," her husband said. "She could have done worse."

"I suppose. What's your daughter's name, darling?"

"Andrea."

"Ooh, nice. Isn't that a nice name, Nat?"

"Very nice."

"Your parents must be delighted to have a grandchild."

"Yes," Susan answered simply, wanting off the subject.

She stayed as long as it took to drink one cup of coffee (sipping furiously) and then, as politely as she could, she took her leave, insisting that she had to be home in time to put Andrea to bed.

"Listen," the mother whispered to her at the elevator, "if you know a nice single man for Jennie, don't be bashful about telling her, okay?"

"Okay." Susan blushed.

"You promise?"

"I promise."

Downstairs, in the lobby, Susan noticed that several of the mailboxes had double locks. Another tribute to the angry army.

She walked over to Broadway, still not ready to go home and face Lou's silent wrath. Strolling along, looking vacantly into storefronts, she realized something profoundly true, or so it seemed. Everyone was living with a horror of one sort or another; the Finkelsteins, caught in a hostile island from which they could not escape, Jennie and Susan's mother, alone for the rest of their lives, perhaps Tara, too, Aunt Ida's loss, everyone. But their horrors were explainable. Hers was not.

And then, as if hearing its cue, her horror returned.

She was at the corner of Broadway and Eighty-eighth, heading south, when the pay phone next to her went off.

She startled, looking at it, thinking after a moment that there was no reason to assume anything. And so she crossed the street and continued to stroll, faking nonchalance.

And the ringing stopped.

At the corner of Eighty-seventh, it happened again.

This time she refused even to look at the pay phone.

At Eighty-sixth, there were two. Ringing. Calling to her, unmistakably.

She hurried on.

And at each corner, malevolent and all-seeing, a phone waited for her, charting the course of her return home, letting her know, all too well, that there was no escaping the Silence.

11

It was annoyed with Susan for having its phones removed.

And amused.

The next morning, after Lou and Andrea had left the apartment (he reminded her that he would call the phone company from his office—a gratuitous slap), Susan lingered alone over coffee. It was good to be in the apartment silenced of its people and machines. She found herself staring into the deep burnt umber in her cup, contemplating quitting the job she had won for herself. She simply wasn't up to any more scenes with Maudey, whose solicitousness had an edge of bitch to it, and even Tara, dear Tara, was more an irritant of late than a friend. People demand your best, she reminded herself, rinsing out the cup, seeing the brown turn orange in the tap water. They aren't prepared to endure your problems. Empathy is as erodible as sand.

The doorbell rang, and momentarily she mistook it for the ringing of a now-pulled phone.

It was Abe at the door with a large manila envelope which he held out to her.

"Mail," he said. "Couldn't fit in the box, so I thought I'd bring it up—" and he hesitated that fraction of a second that always meant he was waiting to be thanked, letting it sink in that he'd done a service, and only two hundred and twenty days before Christmas.

"Thanks, Abe," Susan obliged.

The envelope was thick, bulging with its contents. She opened it. Inside were smaller manila envelopes, perhaps fifty of them, all with the same window in them, the same return address.

They were all bills from the phone company.

She overturned them on the kitchen table and, not understanding their significance, looked through them. They were addressed to different people, some in Manhattan, some in the boroughs, all strangers.

And then Susan realized it was a joke. A grim, macabre joke.

The thing was playing with her.

Downstairs, on the street, it continued laughing. Susan had just thrown all the letters into the corner mailbox when she glanced (not wanting to) at the pay phone not ten feet away. Its cord hung down naked, the receiver having been cut off (this time, at least, the vandal had done her a service).

And then, as she watched it, impossibly, it rang.

She was not the only one who saw it; passing nearby as it called to Susan was a young woman pushing a child in a stroller.

They stopped, the woman cocking her head at it, the child doing the same in imitation; then she smiled and said something to the child, who did not understand but laughed anyway.

Susan heard him as she hurried across the street.

One final laugh, before the holocaust.

They were in school, she and Lou, waiting to see Andrea's class perform *The Vikings* (Andrea was to wear one of her parents' sheets and the bathroom shower-curtain cord). For the moment, standing in the lobby with the other parents ("Hi, remember me? Jessica Fryer, my son was Christopher Columbus?") Susan felt the warmth of those familiar moments of quiet happiness. ("Of course, this is Annie, Queen Isabella's mother.") She looked around in the crowd, at the women (most of them remarkably thin if not especially well-dressed) and the men (Lou was still the best looker, with one possible exception, of all the fathers of the historical figures who were upstairs getting into their costumes).

"What's Andrea this time?" a rotund sour-faced mother asked her.

"A Viking grandmother. Timmy?"

"An American Indian with a cold. I just hope he remembers to bring his handkerchief on stage with him."

"Did Indians have handkerchiefs?"

"This one better." And the woman waddled away, presumably to see what roles her son's other competitors were playing.

There was an urn of coffee set up for the parents and Lou poured out two cups for them as Susan (unwilling but unresisting) looked around to see where the phones were. And how many. Her mother arrived, breathless.

"I was on the phone with Ida for over an hour. I finally said 'Look, Ida, if I don't get out of the house right now I'm going to miss Andrea's play,' but she still wouldn't stop talking, the poor thing. Lou, darling, is that coffee for us?"

It occurred to Susan that no matter what the tragedy, life swiftly returns to its former impatience.

Another grandmother whisked Mrs. Goodman away, temporarily, mercifully. Lou also sought the greener pastures of two fathers, one of whom was a lawyer acquaintance of his, and Susan, alone, wandered along the tiled walls of the lobby, looking at the students' artwork. A few pictures *(In Front of My House; A Tipical Day at Camp)* showed such extraordinary promise (their color sense was overwhelming) that they came close to depressing her. She thought she had adjusted to failure better than that, but there were still moments, now just moments, when her dreams came back to her, loud and humiliating.

"Are you going to Paris to study?" someone named Reenie, who believed everything she was told, had asked her in the Barnard lunchroom seventeen years before.

"Oh, I don't know," Susie answered. "Paris has sort of had it. New York's the center of the art world now. And London, of course. I might study in London for a while, or live among the Sioux for a summer. It's incredible how similar their art is to what's going on in the Village today. . . ."

"God, Susie, you're so lucky."

"Am I? How?"

"To have a talent, a *real* talent, is the greatest blessing in the world. All I'm going to do is get a job and wait to get married."

"I don't think I'll ever marry." Susie made an attempt at looking wistful and almost succeeded. "Lovers, perhaps, but husbands? No."

"Your art is your mate," Reenie said, filled to the brim with admiration.

"What a beautiful thing to say, Reenie. You understand. Few do."

"If I had a talent like yours, nothing would get in my way."

"Nothing will. I promise you. Nothing will."

Susan woke from the reverie, warm-cheeked from her self-induced embarrassment, hoping that she'd never run into Reenie on line at the supermarket or picking up Lou's shirts or taking Andrea to the dentist.

The doors of the auditorium were opened by two giddy children (a third tried, but arrived too late to share in the privilege) and the parents shuffled inside, like visiting celebrities, chatting about the school, tuitions, orthodontia, Connecticut versus Fire Island, the things, unlike fine art, that made up Susan's life.

She sat between Lou and her mother and forgot completely her failure the moment Andrea, looking surprisingly pretty in lipstick and talcumed hair, came on stage.

The play was its usual incoherent sweet mess. Some of the children shouted, some spoke their lines to their chests (Andrea among them), one freckled Viking almost lost his costume and spent the second half of the play, hands behind his neck in a mock attitude of casualness, holding it up.

By the time it was over (and the Vikings sailed back in their huge cardboard ship to Norway from America, laden down with knowledge, a deep respect for another people, and, of course, the obligatory corn), Susan was happier than she'd been in weeks—so happy, in fact, that she suggested they all (Lou, her mother, Andrea, her friend whose mother couldn't make the play) go to a local ice cream parlor and celebrate.

Which they did. Andrea, sitting there behind a mound of chocolate sauce with her hair still white (and getting gummy), radiated pride ("Alice forgot her lines twice but I didn't!") and the moment was worth any loss, even the Whitney.

Which is why the package, sitting there in front of their apartment door on their return, suggested no warning to Susan.

"Hey, what's this? An opening-night present?" Lou picked it up, examined the exquisite silk ribbon and Mylar wrapping paper and handed it to Susan.

"Is it for me?" Andrea hollered.

"Don't know, maybe."

They took it into the kitchen, Andrea snatching at it ("Tell me! Tell me!"), and opened it.

Inside, grinning, leering, the black, glossy, anthropomorphic rodent stared at Susan.

"Oh my God, a Mickey Mouse phone!" Andrea said, prancing about. "It *is* for me!"

Later, when Andrea had taken the dreadful thing to her room (denied permission, many times, for it to be installed), Lou turned to Susan, who had made herself a grim martini and was gulping it, staring at the pocked porcelain surface of the kitchen sink, and said, "Don't you see it's a joke? Some shmuck is trying to bug you. The whole thing is a joke, a prank, don't you see that?''

She saw only the pockmarks and her glass, which needed to be refilled.

12

"Susan, Maudey would like to see you." Maudey's secretary smiled briefly and scurried away, having done the dirty deed.

Susan rinsed her brushes slowly, pulling them through a rag so that they would dry pointed, capped several bottles of paint and said a soundless goodbye to the drawing board that seven months before had seemed a banquet table to her. She looked around her cork-tiled wall, at the stats, (the Thanksgiving Meal was there, still lovely), the picture of Andrea and Lou on the Fire Island ferry (their first affluent summer), the print of Hopper's "Sheridan Square Theater," a photograph of an office party (Tara and she, in mirrored positions, the Tweedledee and Tweedledum of the art department).

She knew Maudey would handle the whole thing beautifully, as indeed she did.

Maudey's office (the purposeful disarray, the

needlepoint pillows always out of place, the horse photographs everywhere and just the right number of ribbons, displayed offhandedly) had briefly been something for Susan to strive for: if not an artist, she would be a power. Now it was another failure.

Maudey, behind her desk, smiled as Susan entered. Smiled and pushed backward away from the desk to assume a position of fraudulent ease.

"Come in, Susan," she said, and Susan noticed with admiration the mixture of friendliness and sorrow in her voice. The burden of power.

"Sit down, dear." And Susan, a child before the principal, obeyed.

It was done with amazing speed, considering how difficult it was for Maudey to let anyone go; indeed, the woman had postponed this inevitable meeting out of her own guilt and distaste for what she had to do, and her feelings for Susan. It was like turning on a friend, betraying a lover, disrespecting a parent. But Maudey was a pawn in the hands of others; she would regret this meeting deeply for a long time.

In five minutes, Susan was out.

Tara said nothing when Susan told her. She got up from her drawing board, painted a mustache on the woman she had been drawing (sweet but useless) and took Susan in her arms.

"Let's go to lunch," she said.

"It's only eleven."

"Fuck 'em."

They went to a small Japanese restaurant in the west fifties, sandwiched between apartment houses, normally crowded but empty at that hour. The waiter, who had a feeble grasp of English, thought they were making a reservation for later, but then was convinced they meant to eat now. He showed them to a table in the rear, after looking around briefly, as if his line of vision was impaired by the many customers.

Then, after they had sipped their martinis for a moment, Tara said (with genuine sadness—the discrepancy between hers and Maudey's was almost comical), "How long?"

"Two weeks, if I want them."

"God, Susan, what am I going to do without you?"

"Just what you used to do, I guess—" and she saw that Tara had taken that the wrong way. "I'll miss you, too."

"Yeah, sure."

"I will. Stop looking like that."

Tara smiled faintly and went back to her martini.

"Look, we're not at the border of Russia with me emigrating to the new world. I still live in New York."

"Sure, sure. So did Thelma Johnston." Tara finished her drink and signaled the waiter.

"Who's Thelma Johnston?" Susan hurried with hers.

"We used to work together at Fawcett. *Un autre, s'il vous plaît.*"

"Lunch?" The waiter, all teeth, grinned.

"Not till the buzz arrives. Two more," she pointed at their empty glasses and he understood, hurrying away through the mob in his imagination.

"What happened to her?"

"Dunno. We had two ladies' lunches and an evening at the ballet. You lose track, you know?"

"Not us, nitwit."

"Says you. Honest, Susan—" and the grin and the moment were evident in her eyes—"what's going to become of me without you? I'll actually get some work done," and then, grabbing her chest, "Jesus, I may even have to go to lunch with Gertrude! *Garçon*, make that a double."

Their second martinis arrived ("Lunch now?" "Lunch later." "I bring menus?" "You keep menus."), and the mood flowed from restrained despair to unalloyed giddiness.

". . . We'll have to make you a care package," Tara was saying as she plucked Susan's olive away from her, "Magic Markers, brushes, pads . . ."

"Petty theft is the opiate of the white-collar worker."

"I'll drink to that. Hey, you think you could get the Xerox in your purse?"

"Bit by bit. It might take a while, though."

"Fine by me."

"You think Maudey would get suspicious if I came back every day for, say, a year?"

"Fuck Maudey."

"If nobody else wants to, why should I?"

They huddled.

"You think she's gay?"

"That would be the least of her problems."

"What do you think she does with that horse of hers? Have you noticed all the research material on Catherine the Great in her office?"

"Why?"

"Susan, everyone knows that Catherine the Great was trampled to death by a horse that she had mount her."

"What?"

"Keep it to yourself."

A third round of martinis found them suddenly

tired and sullen. The waiter, weaving his way toward them, this time through filled tables, carried two menus with a look of such determination that Tara noticed it clear across the room.

"You hungry?" she asked.

"Nope."

"Menus." The waiter thrust one toward Tara, no teeth on display this time.

"I'll have veal Parmesan," she said, refusing it.

"What?"

"Veal Parmesan."

"No veal Parmesan. Sushi, tempura . . ."

"Isn't this an Italian restaurant?" Tara said, and the waiter looked to Susan for help.

"Sushi, tempura, sashimi . . ."

"Sorry—" and Tara stood up— "I never eat Chinese food."

Susan walked Tara back to the office but didn't enter the building with her.

"I'm going to play hookey," she said, embracing her.

"When will we three meet again?"

"In the morning."

"Promise?"

"Promise."

"Go quickly and don't look back."

Which is exactly what Susan did.

Walking home (it gave her an odd, pleasant sensation, not having to race home to her other job), Susan lingered in front of the window of Sam Goody's, wondered who Kiss was, and whether Patti Page was old and fat *(I saw the harbor lights, they only told me we were parting . . .)*, bought a Sabrett (she was hungry, after all) and swam downstream through the packed school of executive salmon, all hurrying back to their offices to spawn corporate decisions. Like Maudey's. *(Fish gotta swim, Maudey gotta fire . . .)* She was aware that she was, if not precisely drunk, not capable of driving a tractor trailer at that moment. And certainly not capable of caring whether or not September's *Home Cooking* had her pumpkin pie on its cover.

But she would miss Tara. Badly.

And Jennie? Jennie was back in Washington. She had gotten used to missing her years ago. ("Tara, meet Jennie, Jennie, Tara.")

She crossed Fifty-ninth Street against the light, (a cab materialized solely to berate her) and chose to finish her holiday by walking home through the park, the memory of her dead squirrel only subliminally advising against it.

The air, sweet, a hint of summer, added to the gin, and Susan found herself heading resolutely to the zoo; it had been years since it was a regular stop on Andrea's outings (zoo, carousel, Rumpelmayer's). Now that she was the mother of a sophisticated eight-year-old, the zoo, puppet shows, so many pleasures were out of bounds. But this time, on her holiday, the choice was hers, and the zoo was the choice.

The seals were the first stop, as always (start at the top and work down). There were three, one male, lazy and sluggish on the rocks, two females, careening through the water like torpedoes, surfacing to look amid the faces for their feeder, disappearing again. She remembered signing a petition years ago to stop the slaughter of seals; it gave her an odd feeling of belonging. The others standing around the fenced pool were tourists; she had a vested interest.

Then the gorilla, sitting with shriveled crossed legs, looking back at everyone as if he knew something they didn't. He glanced at Susan and left the outside cage, hobbling inside, his naked rump held high, as if in derision.

The lioness did the same; took one lazy look at Susan and disappeared within.

And the cheetah.

It occurred to her (an amusing thought, nothing more) that she was downright unpopular with the animals today.

And then the antelopes, usually unresponsive to any but their own innermost thoughts, made the joke a worry. They were hobbling around their small enclosure (had she once also signed a petition to have the cement flooring ripped out?) when one sniffed the air, turned its head to stare at her (it wasn't her imagination; it did look directly at her) and then, as if it had given an inaudible warning to the others, all hurried inside.

And Susan remembered the squirrel, so strangely fond of her, and the second squirrel, floating dead in the pool at the Frick.

She left the park and walked up Fifth Avenue, growing despondent. Animals have a sixth sense, or so many people said. What would Yuri make of it? Would he have a word for it? ("It's not a portent of doom," he would say. "What about the squirrel?" "A coincidence." "And Jimmy?")

At Seventy-second Street, she turned east (it was a little after three), thinking she might walk up Madison and look in the gallery windows to dispel what was fast becoming a foul mood.

It worked, as always. The new artists were clever, several enormously so, but nowhere in her reactions was that special thrill of spotting a genius, a voice. But they were clever, damn them.

She wandered on, feeling a mixture of jealousy and condescension, trying to be kind, failing, until she reached Eighty-sixth Street, crowded with shoppers and schoolchildren. She glanced at her watch; a little after four. Andrea would already be home, ignored by Mrs. Diamond. She remembered her own afternoons at home with her mother, and hurried to a crosstown bus and her daughter.

"Can you be home tomorrow morning?" Lou asked over dinner. "They're going to install the phone." He purposely avoided looking at Susan.

"I can be home permanently." She turned to Andrea. "Eat a few beets, honey. They're good for you."

"Don't like beets."

"I know, but eat a few, anyway."

"What's that supposed to mean?" And Lou continued to look at his plate.

"I've been fired," was all that she said.

"They taste awful."

"I know but they have vitamins in them."

"I take vitamins in the morning."

"And some at night, too. Come on," and she spooned a beet into her daughter's unwilling mouth. "Chew it, Andrea. It won't dissolve."

"How come?" Lou finally looked at her.

What to answer? Susan loathed telling him the real reason: that she was fighting an evil force (alone, with no help from anyone, including him), and that left little time for things as dispensable as jobs. No, that answer would only lead to a hurt silence and, inevitably, to an argument.

"Hard times," she said (nothing more would be necessary at this moment, in a world filled with them).

"I'm sorry," he said but he didn't look it. "Do you mind?"

"Not really. Andrea, chew already."

They didn't speak of it again and Susan, angry, spiteful (rightfully so), pretended she had forgotten to get dessert and left the eclairs in the refrigerator, where no one ever went without first asking her to fetch whatever it was they wanted. She would have hers later, alone.

The evening weighed heavily on her; Lou sat in the kitchen going over a movie contract ("Let him see the eclairs. I hope he sees them"), and Andrea settled down, as always, before the television set, having begged to be allowed to stay up late and see a science fiction movie on Home Box Office (the price: three beets).

Susan, in the bedroom, moved the single night table to Lou's side of the bed (where the intruder, the phone, would sit), tried to read, gave it up, and took a hot bath.

As she lay there in the hot water, drifting, counting her disappointments (her mother had warned her against that, possibly because it usurped her position as court complainer), Susan's mind went back to other, better times.

They were in Florence, she and Lou, walking on the Ponte Vecchio, arms around each other, in shirtsleeves and jeans, looking young and American and cocky, reveling in their love and faultless future. What incredible power had brought the two of them (just the perfect two) together? Lou could finish her every sentence; she could sense his moods before they were fully on him.

They strolled up the Arno, making jokes in broken Italian, pinching each other's bottoms (they were still not used to each other's bodies after two years of marriage) being honestly, frantically in love. And then they went back to the *pensione*, and Lou was inside her, taking her, owning her, being her.

Lying there in the water, she thought of Jennie. Jennie, who might never know what it was like to be loved like that. ("If you know a nice single man for Jennie, don't be bashful about telling her.") But then, of course, she was being foolish. Jennie might have known it many times. Just because she was single didn't mean she was always alone. Things change. Lovers change. They sit at kitchen tables reading contracts, withholding themselves, forgetting intimacy, forgetting *you*.

Once more filled with self-pity, Susan left Florence, (the Arno, like her bath water, ended up in a sewer) and toweled herself dry. She wiped the mist from the medicine-chest mirror and took a harsh look at herself. She had been pretty, almost beautiful, a little while ago. She was still attractive (smart eyes, her father had always said), but middle age was there around the eyes, coming out at the corners of her mouth. (Was her nose larger, or was that only an imagined Jewish fear?)

She put on a robe and went into the bedroom, noticing, almost with surprise, that the night table was on the wrong side of the bed. And its clock read quarter after ten.

Way past Andrea's bedtime.

"Oh, my God, are you still up?" she said (of

course she'd still be up; had they kissed goodnight?), entering the living room where Andrea was sitting much too close to the set. ("Honey, it's bad for your eyes," was virtually a nightly chant.)

"A few minutes more, Mommy!" This said with desperation.

"All right, but only a few."

She settled down on the couch, drawing Andrea away from the set, closer to her. She listened for the sound of the refrigerator door being opened in the kitchen but heard nothing.

On the set, what appeared to be a spaceship (her jargon; Andrea, quite properly, called them space *vehicles*) was moving through what appeared to be space (this was the new art, special effects; was *everything* about her obsolete?) at a dizzying speed. All hands seemed frantic (the usual frenzy of actors trying not to smile). Susan watched, attentive for a moment (that was her usual endurance for space *vehicles*) and admired one of the young actors (no doubt a surfer between film commitments). And then the ship (*vehicle*, damn) careened toward something out there in the starry blackness, something large and without stars, totally black, circular, ominous, magnetic. Too late Susan recognized it as a black hole—she had seen the coming attractions for the film, hated it on sight. Instinctively, she knew she was watching something important, something with great meaning for her, *to* her. Transfixed, she stared at the television set (heart beating faster now, mouth drying so quickly she could feel it). The ship moved closer to the dreadful thing, being sucked in by it, no chance of getting away now, either the actors or her. Then they plunged (and her with them) into the thing, down into its special-effects void, through concentric

circles of blackness, going round and round, dizzy
(she was perspiring), faster, through circle after
circle, screen a jumble of blurred faces and blackness, breathless, frozen time, round and round
and . . .

Susan looked away from the screen, aware that she
was virtually panting.

*What was it? What was this thing that was happen-
ing to her?*

And her eyes sought it out again.

They had gone through the black hole and emerged
somewhere else.

A figure, too squared-off to be a man, too human-
oid to be anything else, was standing atop a craggy
hill. There were other hills in the distance. All
demented. Deformed. Like nothing in this world.
And there were flames rising up between them, a mist
of smoke and ash, an air so thick and dense it defied
breathing.

It was hell.

She was watching hell. An artist's hell but hell
nonetheless.

And suddenly, wretchedly, assuredly, she knew
where her phone calls were coming from.

13

Some part of Susan shut down.

Numbly she put Andrea to bed (no struggle, the child was exhausted) and went to bed herself. There in the darkness she tried to deny the truth briefly but could not; soon she would wake to its full horror, soon the glands that were protecting her would cease to function, that part of her brain that had short-circuited would be repaired and the terror would be on her.

Hell was a reality. (If hell, heaven? God? Could he be called on?)

She considered praying, lying there in her stupor, but how? She had never prayed (not even when it was called for, upstairs in the synagogue; then she had merely daydreamed). Admonishments from her childhood, now with the power of absolute truths, came back to her. *Do not take the Lord's name in vain*. (What did that mean? Not to speak his name? Not to pray?) *God is good, trust Him*. (How, when such undeserved punishments threatened her?)

Were they undeserved? She thought of her brother, murdered in the womb, and she following so closely. (Could she have been conceived before his slaying? Had she done it? Can one fetus destroy another? Wouldn't it be washed away in the same wave of blood?)

She closed her eyes and tried to will herself to sleep; she would need her strength to fight. But behind her lids was the figure of a man standing on a craggy hill amid flames. She opened her eyes quickly, forcing it away.

"Our father, which art in heaven, hallowed be thy name," she whispered. "Thy kingdom come, thy will be done on earth as it is in heaven." She paused, listening, as if for an answer, but none came.

"Please, God," she whispered, "please," and she felt the futility of prayer.

Later, it might have been hours—Susan's perception of time was dulled, like the rest of her senses, by fear—Lou entered the room.

"You asleep?" he said.

Would he help her? Could he?

"No."

"I'm beat." He undressed in the dark. Approaching the bed, he hit against the night table and cursed.

"I moved it for your phone. Sorry."

"It's all right." He slid into bed, the other side of the bed, far from her. "Goodnight."

"Goodnight."

If he knew the truth, as surely as she knew it, would he not withhold himself? Could he be an ally?

"Lou," she said, finally, the decision having taken time.

"Yes?" came back in the darkness.

"Do you believe in hell?"

"Oh, shit, Susan, I'm exhausted." And he turned to face away from her.

She lay there, saying nothing, until dawn.

At a little after nine in the morning (Susan had slept at most an hour and that was fitfully) the man arrived with the phone. She stood there in the bedroom doorway, watching him install it (there would be nowhere to hide now, nowhere to sleep), avoiding his friendly chattiness, and when he was gone (eventually he stopped trying; he left wordlessly) she sat on the bed, staring at the phone, realizing its full potential.

The logic of hell's use of it seemed appropriate; no messenger in the darkness, no tempting devil, no, a simple phone call, the longest of distances, hell worked the way men did.

It rang.

"Don't do this to me," she spoke to it.

And it rang in response.

"Please, I haven't done anything," she pleaded with the shiny black malevolent servant of Satan. "Please!"

Another ring, like a sneer. (What did guilt have to do with it?)

"I have a child!"

And a snicker. (A child? Good. Put her on the phone.)

"God, please, help me!"

And then, mocking her, enjoying her torment,

reveling in it, the separate rings joined together into one endless mechanical laugh.

Susan didn't hear the end of it; she fled the apartment.

Outside in the sunshine (sunshine did exist, therefore God, therefore help, salvation, an end to it), she walked down to Riverside Park (past the castrated pay phone, which did not ring; its silence as powerful —implosion rather than explosion) and sat on a bench.

She prayed.

" . . . If there's something I've done, something I didn't realize was bad, forgive me. Tell me what it was. Please, God. Tell me. Tell me."

An old woman was walking nearby (placing one burdensome foot slowly in front of the other, a parody of walking) and heard her. She turned slowly to Susan (even that was an effort) and smiled. (Did she know it was prayer?) But then, receiving only a helpless look in return for her pains, she cranked her body to face away and continued her careful, endlessly grueling task of walking.

God had not answered; his messenger (if the ancient woman was his messenger) had conveyed nothing but pain; Susan was alone—alone on the outskirts of hell, and hell was beckoning to her.

She left the park and took a bus downtown to the only person who might, if she could be made to realize the full weight of Susan's plight, help her.

Tara sat behind her drawing board (the same sketched woman lying there; the mustache now carefully painted out) listening. And if she disbelieved what she heard, she was generous enough not to let it show. When Susan was finished, staring at the floor, ashamed that these obscenities had to be voiced, Tara took her hands and said, in a voice heavy with concern, "Honey, I didn't know. I never would have been such a shit to you if I'd known."

"I know that."

"Why didn't you tell me what was happening? How bad it was?"

"I couldn't. It sounds so crazy."

"What the hell difference does that make? Whatever it is that's happening to you . . ."

Susan's face instantly showed her disappointment. "I told you what it is."

Tara paused, squeezed Susan's hands in hers and spoke gently but resolutely. "Susan, I'm on your side and I'm going to do whatever I can do to help you get over this thing, but I can't lie to you, not and be any help. I don't believe in hell or God or any of that stuff—" she saw Susan's eyes fill with sorrow—"but it doesn't matter what I think it is. What matters is that I'm on your side come . . ." and she paused.

"Hell or high water?" Susan finished the sentence wryly.

"Rain or shine?" And Tara smiled.

"Thank you."

They held each other's hands silently for a moment, Susan thanking Tara's nonexistent God for her. And then Tara spoke.

"Look, it hasn't harmed you so far, has it?"

"No."

"Then calm down, will you? You look like pieces of you are gonna fly off in all directions. Let's go shopping. Come on, time off for something normal."

Susan nodded yes.

And uptown, on her bed, Sweet William, who had

been sleeping, had a nightmare. His legs, running, trying uselessly to get him out of the dream, moved him to the edge of the bed, Lou's side, and he toppled off it, knocking over the night table.

And the phone.

14

They shopped with a vengeance, Tara quite sure that whatever Susan's problem (emotional, physical, they were the only possibilities), nothing could assuage it as well as a little blatant self-indulgence. They went first to Bloomingdale's, where Tara insisted Susan try on (she almost, but not quite made her buy it) a Saint-Laurent pants suit; then upstairs to housewares and a beautiful but not even remotely useful set of pickle dishes, some Israeli glass goblets that looked like early Tiffany, and finally the silver section, where Susan, worn down by Tara's therapeutic cheer, did spend much too much money on a plated staghorn candlestick ("Susan, it's gorgeous and you're going to have it!"). Then to Alexander's for some serious and sensible *buying* (towels, summer shorts for Andrea, a new swimsuit in case they did get to Fire Island).

At two o'clock, with two respectably filled shopping bags in tow, Susan walked Tara to the office but once again declined to go upstairs with her.

"If I'm fired," she said, feeling better (the shopping had worked), "I'm fired. I may as well go home and make pot roast like every other self-respecting housewife."

"You coming in tomorrow?"

"Dunno."

"Want to go to a movie tomorrow night?"

"Maybe."

"I'll call you." This without thinking.

"Call Lou. It's the same number."

"Be calm and don't forget," Tara called over her shoulder as she climbed the steps in front of their office skyscraper, "spend money!"

Recognizing the wisdom of her words, Susan hailed a cab (move over, Bendel's ladies) and went home.

To it.

The moment she opened the front door, Susan knew something was wrong.

She could hear nothing, but she knew.

She put her bags down in the doorway of the living room, peered in, nothing out of place there, crossed the hall, glanced in the kitchen, the same, and walked down the long central hall to her bedroom.

As she drew near the doorway, she heard it.

The call of hell. The soundless filth.

Her hands went over her ears as she hurried into the room, saw the table upended, the phone, open, live.

She slammed the phone and receiver together quickly like cymbals, cutting it off, out.

And then, sitting on the floor next to the bed (how had it come into her home? When? How long had it been there?), she heard another sound.

A muffled growl.

"Sweet William?" she called out.

The growl continued.

"Sweet William?"

She searched the room for him (his noise never stopped), under the bed, behind a chair, beneath the dresser (the growl, never broken, was her beacon), and then she saw the closet door, slightly ajar.

"Honey, it's okay, I'm home." And she opened the door.

He was lying in the back, behind her shoe rack, coiled there, his mouth and chest drenched with spit, his thin black lips raised, the stained old teeth bared, his ears slammed down on the sides of his head. Lying there, snarling, driven to madness.

He had been there all the while. Forced to listen to it while she and Tara shopped. Biting the air as they laughed. Foaming and moaning as his mistress (who loved him and had led him to this) enjoyed herself.

"Oh, sweetheart," Susan said, almost crying at the sight of him, "it's all right. Mama's home." And she went to touch him.

His teeth, old and brittle though they were, ripped into her hand like spikes.

She leaped backward, out of surprise as much as pain, and the dog sank its head back down into itself, the nonstop growl growing louder for a moment, then back to its former soft chant.

She went into the bathroom and ran cold water over her hand to stop the hurt. There was little blood, small wells of it in the puncture wounds, bruises forming rapidly. And then, mixed with her concern and guilt over Sweet William, she felt anger at Lou for insisting the weapon be brought back into their home. Now he would see she was right; her hand would be the proof.

Her hand would be the least of it.

She turned, the sound of Sweet William's terror louder now, and left the bathroom. Stepping into the bedroom, she saw him. He had come out of the closet, his head slung low, hanging there cocked, staring at her with demented eyes, teeth showing, brown and spotted, spittle hanging down in threads, the hair on his back standing straight up in clumps.

"Sweet William . . ." she said, and his jaws opened in response, the snarl gagging him for a moment. "Sweet William," she repeated, entreated, and his head sank lower, his lips pulled higher to expose the teeth.

She tried for the doorway, slowly, but he saw her intent and was there first, no longer a dog, now a demon, enjoying her fear.

"Sit, boy," she said, and he snarled, taking his first step toward her, head lowered for the attack.

"Sweet William, listen to me!" And she backed up toward the bathroom door, still ajar.

He circled her quickly, snarling, gagging, cutting her off from the exit.

"Sweet William, it's me!"

He lunged forward, teeth biting together, inches from her leg. Susan stepped back quickly, felt the bed behind her, lifted herself on to it, legs out of reach of the teeth.

"Sit, boy! Sit!"

He came up to the bed, stood on it, front paws only, his spit falling on it in droplets. He lunged for her again. She moved backward, against the wall.

"Sweet William, it's me! Stop it!"

In one movement he was on the bed and he drove his teeth into her leg. They screamed together, she from the pain, he from the frenzy of attack.

"God!" She pulled him off her, and with the strength pain had given her, hurled him off the bed.

He hit the floor, yelped, and was on the bed again, teeth bared, showing her blood on them.

Susan leaped from the bed and was across the room, almost to the door, before she heard Sweet William hit the floor, another yelp, and felt his teeth in her ankle.

She pulled herself and him to the door and prying his jaws apart, crying, shouting, "Stop it! Stop it!" threw him backward and slammed the door on him.

She sat on the floor of the hallway, looking at her leg (bright red), listening to his growls coming from under the door and then the sound of his nails as he tried to dig his way back to her.

She washed the leg in Andrea's bathroom (the wounds, though painful, were merely punctures) and wrapped a towel around it as a makeshift bandage. Carefully sponging up the droplets of blood (on the tub, the floor, even spattered halfway up the sink) lest they frighten Andrea, she tried to decide what to do. To call the police (*call?* She amended it to *get*) would mean Sweet William's death, and frightened of him though she was, she loved him. He hadn't attacked her; it was that thing lying there spewing its venom. No, Sweet William was its victim as surely as she was. The *first* victim, she thought, and avoided the implications of that thought.

Then there was a crash, shattering glass.

She went to the bedroom door and listened. Had he broken something in his frenzy? Lamp, mirror, bathroom glass?

No sound.

"Sweet William?" She pressed her ear against the door. "Sweet William?"

Nothing.

Slowly, pressing her body against the door, prepared to slam it shut if need be, she opened it.

One of the windows was broken, shards of glass protruding from its corners pointing to the jagged hole in the middle.

The hole through which Sweet William had hurled himself to the cement, eleven stories down, rather than attack his beloved mistress again.

Tara arrived at the apartment shortly after nine, having called and been told. Susan was lying on the living room couch, a true bandage on her leg. (Lou had put it there though she refused to speak to him other than to say, "It's your fault. I told you it would happen!")

"I don't want him in here," Susan said as Lou brought Tara in.

"Honey . . ."

"I don't want him in here!" And Lou, hesitating for a moment, weighing his own guilt and anger, chose the latter and slammed out of the room to his bedroom.

"What on earth happened?" Tara saw the pink spotted gauze on Susan's leg and ankle.

"He was my puppy—" and Susan held a pillow in front of her face and wept, suddenly and deeply, into it. "He never hurt a thing. He wouldn't even chase squirrels in the park, he was so gentle. . . ." (And her own squirrel, floating face down in the pool at the Frick, came back to her.) "It starts with animals. If they get too close to me—" the logic was unassailable to her—"it kills them. At the zoo the animals knew it. They were afraid to look at me!"

"Honey, calm down." Tara took her injured hand in her own, only then seeing the wounds.

"I'm marked, Tara! I'm marked by hell!" Her uncontrollable sobs prevented any further speech or thought.

Tara had to ask Lou where they kept their gin, and as they stood alone in the kitchen (Susan lay in the other room, whimpering now), she asked him, "Is she still seeing her shrink?"

"She says she is." And as he mixed the gin and vermouth, he added bitterly, "She says a lot of things."

"What do you think made the dog do it?"

He looked at her, at his wife's friend (not his) and handed her the drink. "He was probably protecting himself."

Tara thought it was a disgusting thing to say, even if his wife wouldn't speak to him. Even if it was true. She took the martini to Susan without saying another word to Lou.

"Here, honey, drink this."

Susan accepted it gladly and felt comforted by the burning in her throat—a sensation she normally disliked—for she knew that after it followed, if not peace, at least some pharmacological calm.

"I'm not crazy, Tara. I'm not."

"No one said you were."

"No one had to say it. It's all over your face. And his. God, Tara, I think I hate him!"

"No, you don't. You're just angry with him—"

and she thought of his hateful remark. "You're both going through a rough period."

"What am I going to do?" And then, at that moment when calm was so desperately needed, a thought far more horrendous than any so far came to her: What if Andrea had been home when the phone was off the hook?

Tara stayed with her until midnight, by which time Susan, lulled by gin, thought she might be able to sleep. She showed Tara to the door, locked it and went into the kitchen. From a drawer she removed a large pair of scissors (their heaviest) and quietly walked to her bedroom.

Lou was sleeping under an extra blanket, the cardboard he had taped to the window only partially cutting out the cool night air.

She walked quietly around to his side of the bed and looked at him.

Did she indeed hate him?

She knelt on the floor beside him.

Is it possible to hate someone you've loved? To truly hate him?

Yes, she decided it was.

And with that, she sliced through the phone cord, leaving his weapon impotent.

15

The first vague awareness Susan had that she was awake was that she was cold. She drew the blankets up around her face; they felt thicker than normal. She half opened her eyes and saw the color scarlet (what could that be?) and slowly remembered the scarlet blanket, a spare, she kept in the hall closet. Lou must have covered her with it. (Why? She recalled, dimly, something about the window being open.)

She liked this feeling of being unfocused; she frequently lingered within it, before letting her thoughts pull together into assignments (get Lou and Andrea up. Make breakfast. Walk S. W.).

She wiggled a foot under the blanket at the thought of Sweet William and waited for him to pounce on it, catlike (their favorite morning game).

He didn't.

The throbbing in her head and the cloudy feeling

of nausea (far off, coming closer) brought everything back to her now and she closed her eyes tight against it. Lying there, trying to fall asleep again, knowing that she wouldn't, Susan wished, for one brief moment, that she would never wake again.

She opened her eyes to find the bedroom filled with sunlight. For a moment she assumed it had something to do with the broken window, but then, glancing at the clock on the dresser, she realized it was after ten. (The sun never shone into their bedroom until it cleared the building across the street, shortly before ten.) Lou's side of the bed was empty; that didn't surprise her. After last night, he would sulk off to his office, glad to be rid of her.

She sat up, felt the hangover (this one would doubtless be a beauty) and slowly went into the bathroom, not looking at the window lest the whole nightmare return before she could deal with it.

Standing at the bathroom sink, swallowing aspirins, (why could she never remember to take them the night before and spare herself this sickness?), she saw her dried blood spots and remembered cleaning Andrea's bathroom.

A new anger. Why hadn't Lou let Andrea kiss her goodbye?

It wasn't until her second cup of coffee that she decided Lou had left quietly so that she could sleep undisturbed. She would have dwelled on that guilt if the doorbell hadn't rung.

"Morning." The superintendent looked distressed, but then he always looked distressed when speaking to the tenants, all of whom he feared.

Susan remembered how he avoided her eyes when they carried Sweet William into the basement and left him (what had once been him) in the storage room.

"What do you want us to do with the dog?" he asked, when Susan offered no response.

They had laid him on his side on the cold cement floor.

"I don't know."

They hadn't bothered to cover him; it never occurred to them.

"We can't leave him there."

He looked like he was sleeping; as if at any moment, he'd wake and stretch his head forward to be kissed.

"No . . . no, of course not."

Or roll over, huge legs dangling in the air, whining to be scratched.

"The garbage men said they can't take him. . . ."

"No, please don't let them. . . ."

"It's against the law. . . :"

"Yes, I realize, I just don't know at this moment. . . ."

"We can't leave him there. . . ."

Finally it was arranged that the superintendent would call Lou at his office ("Can't we call him now?" "No, our phone is out of order") and convey the message that Susan wanted Sweet William buried.

Thus brutalized once more, Susan dressed and left the apartment to seek comfort in the way she always had—by doing menial tasks. (When Andrea, at two, had a violent ear infection, Susan had scrubbed the kitchen till it dazzled.) On Amsterdam Avenue she found a glazier who promised to come to the apartment between two and three. (No small victory, this; they usually made you wait all afternoon.) Then she opted to do her marketing in several small shops, rather than at the supermarket where it was joyless, went to a hardware store for unneeded supplies, and finally, having run out of fake errands, returned home.

The superintendent was in the lobby as she entered the building; she hurried to the elevator to avoid him.

"Mrs. Reed—" he caught up to her before she could press her button, and unwillingly she placed her foot against the door to keep it open.

"Yes?"

"I spoke to your husband." His voice was hushed (embarrassment? reverence?). "Somebody's coming by this afternoon."

"Thank you." She removed her foot.

"Oh, and the telephone man was here."

The door was closing as he said it; she had to jump to hit the "door open" button.

"What telephone man? I didn't send for any telephone man."

His face, always apologetic before the tenants, appeared stricken.

"He said you did. I only let him in because you said your phone was out of order . . ." and Susan pressed her floor button, leaving him standing there pleading his innocence.

Upstairs, she entered the apartment quickly, stopping first in the kitchen to rid herself of her packages.

The white wall phone, new, glistened at her.

And in the living room, on the table where a phone had always been, a new one sat.

And, the worst mockery of all, in the bedroom, Lou's phone, repaired, sat on her side of the bed.

"You can't do this to me!" she screamed.

And they answered.

She stood there, in the bedroom, hearing their metallic jeers echo throughout the apartment, knowing that they would win, would always win, no matter what she did, no matter where she went, no matter what unlistening God condescended to help her.

And stubbornly, she got the shears from the kitchen drawer and silenced them all.

Later, when she was napping (exhausted, always exhausted) grotesquery was added to grotesquery. She was awakened by the sound of the phones.

They had healed themselves.

16

Days went by in silent despair now, Susan waiting, watching for a sign of the next attack, the phones sitting quietly, always in reach of her.

One afternoon, when there was no more housework she could conjure up (the kitchen cupboards were relined, the closets put in order, even Andrea's toys were organized shelf by shelf), Susan went back to the office to pick up her things.

There was genuine sadness on seeing her. (Because she had been fired, or had Tara told them?)

"We're gonna miss you, kid," one of the art directors said as she headed down the long hall of offices to her own. She stopped briefly to acknowledge the kindness.

"I'll miss you, too, Bud. And your dirty jokes."

"I'll call them in to you," he answered.

"Mail them." And there was no hint on his face that Tara had said anything.

Her own cubicle seemed foreign to her; the illustration she had been working on was gone, probably handed over to someone else to finish, the drawing board tidy (it never had been when it belonged to her).

Slowly she removed her possessions. The pictures, a loving cup that read "Hausfrau of the Year" (Tara had given it to her when she refused to leave Lou and Andrea to spend a weekend with her at her parents' upstate retreat), a transistor radio (useless, transmitting only static in the windowless interior).

And then she looked up and saw Tara standing in the doorway, looking at her as if she might cry.

"Hi," Tara said.

"Hi, yourself."

"Collecting your junk?"

"Uh-huh."

"Mind if I crawl into the package?"

"Love it."

Tara came into the cubicle and plopped herself, as always, on the drawing board.

"Guess what?" she said.

"What?"

"I'm fellaless again."

"What's that mean?"

"It means that Yuri found a lady orthopedist with a private practice and forty-inch tits."

"I'm sorry," Susan said but her sympathy was lessened for recognizing that Tara's sadness was not about her leaving.

"Yeah, well, once an old maid . . ."

Susan's resentment didn't last long; she put her arm around Tara and shook her. "Anybody who puts out as much as you do is no old maid. . . ."

"So I'm a promiscuous old maid."

"Wanna cut out early and get bombed?"

Tara cocked her pretty head, considering it. "I've got a ton of work to do."

"Do it tomorrow."

She turned to Susan, smiled, glanced around (seeing the result of too many missed days) and said, "You're on."

They crossed the street to the Warwick bar and ordered their customary martinis, settling in comfortably in a corner, preparing to mourn, in their separate ways, their separate griefs.

"I really liked him," Tara was saying when their drinks had arrived and the time for regrets was right. "And goddamn it, I was so good to him. I really was, Susan. I didn't pull any of my usual shit on him. I was practically normal, for crissake. What the hell do they *want*?" And her voice rose so that a bartender glanced over at her.

"I don't know. Probably more of the same."

"I mean, a lady orthopedist! Is that someone for a grown man?" She laughed. "But enough about me. How's it going?"

Susan shrugged and ate her olive.

"That bad?"

"Not good." And she told her about the phones, the three intruders waiting for her at home.

"Maybe Lou had them installed," Tara said, looking for an explanation, any explanation.

"It isn't Lou." Susan stared at a small eddy on the surface of her drink. "You know what it is."

"I don't know anything." And then, suddenly and with enough emotion to cause another glance from the bartender, "Susan, things like that don't happen."

"Don't they? How do you know?"

"I just do."

"Yes." Susan touched the top of the viscous liquid, causing it to rise to meet her finger. "I knew it, too, before."

They calmed (or rather, Tara calmed, for Susan was beyond excitation) and eventually, when there was no more to say, either about the phones or Yuri, Tara said, with a sudden despair, "How am I going to get in touch with you?"

"Call," Susan answered. "I'm never far from a phone."

Several days later, Tara did call.

Susan was with Andrea, as she always was since dismissing Mrs. Diamond. Their evenings were filled with each other, the television set fading rapidly into the background. Susan did indeed teach her to paint (as her mother claimed to have taught her). She taught her perspective ("Make the one in the background smaller, honey. That's right. As things get farther away they get smaller. . . .") and balance and figure drawing. She seemed filled with a need to be with her daughter, to express her love for her, to absorb her and be absorbed in case she was suddenly missing (like Susan's father, who had left without really having been there).

Lou came into Andrea's room a moment after Susan heard the phone ring.

"It's Tara. Will you talk to her?" he asked, knowing her answer.

"No."

He left the room and Andrea looked up from the watercolor of a house that they had been working on.

"Are you mad at Tara, Mommy?"

"No, dear. I'd just rather be with you than talk on

the phone." She caressed her daughter's hair.

Andrea added a dog to the lawn outside the house. A large, fat dog.

"Sweet William," the child said. "He's not dead."

"No, dear. Not to us," and she went into her bedroom in time to see Lou hang up the phone.

"She says to come to her apartment tomorrow night. It's important," he said, and then rolled over, back toward her, to face the television set.

Susan stared at his back for a moment (it had been days since the silence between them started) and went back to Andrea.

"It's beautiful," she said, looking at the picture, recognizing her own lack of talent. "It's beautiful and you're the most beautiful girl in the world."

"No, I'm not," Andrea said matter-of-factly.

"Yes, you are." And she took her daughter in her arms with more emotion than she wished to show. "You're the most beautiful thing I've ever seen in all my life."

"Okay," Andrea acceded, squirming out of her grasp.

The next evening, shortly after eight, Susan climbed the steps in front of Tara's brownstone and entered the lobby. She could smell spaghetti sauce coming from within as she stood before the locked inner door (again, the angry army had to be kept out) and rang Tara's intercom bell.

"Yeah?" Tara's voice called.

"It's me." The buzzer sounded.

Inside, climbing the stairs, the smell of sauce was beautiful and lessened only as she passed the second floor, where it was replaced by the smell of homebaked bread. Susan momentarily envied these people who could eat their dinners so late; by eight uptown, dishes were done and children bathed, husbands settled before their TV sets and the humdrumness started.

Tara's head appeared at the top of the final flight of stairs.

"Hup two three four," she said.

"God, I wish you'd get an elevator—" but Susan didn't mean it. The stairs, the smells, the freedom were all perfect.

"So, what's important?" Susan asked as Tara poured her a glass of wine.

"The pillows. Nice?"

Susan sat forward on the couch and looked behind her. She recognized it was Tara's new matching pillows that had been making her uncomfortable.

"Gorgeous. Now, what's important?"

"Sweetheart—" she handed her the wine— "what I've been through for you. Cheers."

They sipped.

"What? Will you tell me?"

"Don't rush me. . . ." And Susan echoed the inevitable "I'll work cheaper."

"I've been through hell." Tara, realizing what she had said, added, "Metaphorically, to get in touch with someone from the phone company, and I finally found someone. She's a friend of a friend of a friend, but I spoke with her last night and she's coming over here to talk to you. . . ."

"Whatever for?" Susan felt a rush of impatience; she was surrounded by people for whom only the rational was possible. What help could another one be?

"Because I called the phone company and pretended this thing was happening to me and they laughed in my face. . . .''

"I could have told you that, Tara."

"Yeah, but Harriet didn't laugh. That's her name, Harriet Walgreen. She was really concerned. . . .''

"God, here we go again—" and Susan rearranged the hateful pillows out of her way. "First a psychic stud, then a telephone operator . . .''

"She happens to be vice-president of Ma Bell, so watch your mouth. And you're damn right, here we go again. And we'll keep on going until this thing is over, or would you like to spend the rest of your life hiding every time the phone rings?" Tara said angrily, forcing a brief silence.

"Do many people say thank you by biting your head off?" Susan apologized.

"Not many." And to lighten the mood she added, "You don't like the pillows?"

"I love the pillows."

"They're uncomfortable?"

Susan laughed (the first time in days). "I love you."

"Yeah, a lot of good it does me. Can you grow a penis?"

"I can't even grow a plant."

At eight-thirty, precisely as arranged, the intercom buzzed and Tara announced that Harriet was on her way up.

"I hope she's not too old for the stairs," Susan said.

She was not. Harriet Walgreen was, like Tara, several years younger than Susan and absolutely stunning. (Where does Tara dig them up? Susan thought.) In addition to beauty (a mane of honey-colored hair, an astonishing smile) she had what secretaries at their office (Tara's office now) called "style." Even casually dressed as she was, one could, if one were a woman, smell the faint and delicious odor of money about her.

All of which would have put Susan off her instantly if Harriet hadn't also been deeply sympathetic.

"I've been spooked all day over it," she said behind her Scotch and water (it occurred to Susan that she and Tara, with their cheap white wine, were infinitely tacky in comparison). "I actually locked myself in my office and had a joint." Her smile radiated without the least hint of self-consciousness.

"Got another?" Tara asked.

"Menthol or regular?" She reached into her purse (alligator—Susan almost salivated) and withdrew one.

They lit up, passing the joint among them frequently until the tension of their meeting was replaced by a warm glow of friendship.

"You do believe me?" Susan asked.

"Of course—" and for a moment Susan thought, There is someone else who knows the truth—but Harriet quickly dispelled that. "I believe that someone's calling you." She looked apologetic.

"Well, that will have to do." Susan, mellowed by the wine and marijuana, wasn't up to pushing the point.

"I checked on the new phones that were installed," Harriet went on, to prove her intent to help.

"I told her," Tara said, holding in her breath and the smoke.

"There was no order for them and no record of their having been installed."

"Of course not." Susan leaned back and closed her eyes, drifting. "And no record of their reinstalling themselves."

"Shit," Harriet said softly. "It's too much."

"Much too much. Tara, pass the joint already."

"When do the calls come?"

"When I'm alone." (When Sweet William was alone.)

"Do they come at any regular time?"

"No. Whenever."

"Shit."

They lit another joint, faced with the apparent helplessness of their now mutual problem (it occurred to Susan that Harriet was an extraordinarily nice woman, but then, why shouldn't she be, looking like that?).

"You're really a doll to try to help me," Susan said suddenly, loudly, the marijuana lifting her onto a new, more excitable plateau.

"A doll," Harriet parroted and then started to laugh. "My mother used to use that word."

"A regular doll," Tara said and she started to giggle.

Paranoia hit Susan, but only briefly, and then she joined them in their drugged giddiness.

"He makes a good living," she said, to laughing approval.

"He comes from money," someone else said. "Money, Ohio."

"She's a regular person."

"Don't keep yourself strange!" (At that, the three of them guffawed.)

Later, when the giddiness had passed and was replaced by a somber melancholy, Harriet turned to Susan and said earnestly, "I'm going to have a trace put on your phone, Susan."

"My God, just like in the movies," Tara, wishing the giddiness to return, said.

"Will you?"

"Uh-huh."

"Thank you—" and it occurred to her that it wouldn't do any good. "What if the calls can't be traced? If they come from someplace you can't trace?"

"That's impossible."

"What if it happens?"

"We'll find you an exorcist." She saw the painfully lonely look on Susan's face. "It's impossible, honey."

"So was the *Titanic*."

"Look, let's have lunch tomorrow and talk about it. Meanwhile, somebody help me find my feet. If I'm late one more night, Larry'll kill me."

"Who's Larry?"

"My *hubby*. The one who comes from money." She struggled to her feet. "One o'clock, the Maison Française on Fifty-sixth, okay?"

Susan also had difficulty climbing out of the couch (where she was wadded in among Tara's damned matching pillows). She took Harriet's hand warmly and wanted to say something important.

"Thank you," was all that came out.

Later, when Harriet was gone, Tara was the first to verbalize what they both had been thinking.

"When I grow up, I want to be her."

"I'd settle for being her purse." And briefly, at least, life was normal.

*   *   *

At one o'clock the following day Susan entered La
Maison Française, mentioned Harriet's name to the
head waiter and was shown to their table.

"May I get you a drink?" The waiter seemed
decidedly subservient, embarrassing her. (Had it
been Susan's usual table instead of Harriet's, she
knew he would have been normally curt.) She
ordered a Scotch and water (imitation being the
sincerest form) and settled in to wait for Harriet.

"God, that's a gorgeous suit," Harriet said as she
slid onto the banquette next to Susan. "Sorry I'm
late. Where'd you get it?"

"Saks," Susan answered, pleased that she had
taken great pains in dressing. (Harriet's outfit was,
of course, a classic.) "And yours?"

"Ralph Lauren, but don't hate me for it. It was a
present from Larry. We ate in for two weeks to pay
for it. Hi, Joseph." The waiter, unasked, brought
her drink, placing it before her with a warm smile of
admiration. "How did Edward like the Yankee
game?"

"Loved it, Miss Walgreen. Thanks again."

"Well—" Harriet raised her glass to toast Susan.
"Congratulations. You've now got a tapped phone."

"Already?"

"We don't kid around at Ma Bell."

"What part of heaven do you come from?" Susan
asked, overwhelmed by her new friend's kindness.
(When it was over, if it was ever over, they would be
friends; Susan would then have the courage to ask
Harriet's advice on dressing, hair style, living,
breathing.)

"The part that's in Brooklyn."

"You're kidding."

"Nope, but I worked at it. Christ, did I work at it—" and she toasted herself. "I was so stoned last night . . ."

"Me, too."

"When I got home, I ate everything in the refrigerator including the ice cubes and then I attacked Larry."

"Was he stoned too?"

"He doesn't have to be. Thank God I married a sex maniac."

Susan thought of Lou, sleeping far from her on his side of the bed; how long had it been since she attacked him?

"Listen," Harriet said, suddenly businesslike, "we've got to do some planning. The next time he calls you . . ."

"He?"

"He, it, them, whatever, I want you to stay on the phone as long as possible. . . ."

"Harriet, I can't," and she saw Sweet William, once again in the back of her closet, shivering, snarling, mad. "Even a moment of it terrifies me."

"Susan, we can't trace the call if you hang up. Look, put the phone down and get out of the room, but don't hang up. That's important, *don't hang up.*"

"All right," she agreed, reluctantly.

"Also, when I want to reach you, I'll ring once, then hang up and redial so you'll know it's me."

"It won't do any good, Harriet. It can cut you off." And the uselessness of her plan, of any mere human's plan, was painfully evident.

"Do it anyway, okay?"

"Okay."

"And stop looking so sad. We'll get him. Nothing can beat Ma Bell. That's what's so nice about being a monopoly. Now, you like *coq au vin?*"

They ate without further reference to Susan's caller, and Harriet, cheerful and secure, almost succeeded in making her feel the same.

For a while, at least.

17

Susan rented a car and drove to Long Island to the pet cemetery where Sweet William had been buried. She was surprised at the size of it, large and sprawling as any human version, gracefully sculptured and serene. Years before, she would have laughed at the thought that all this beauty was created for the corpses of dogs and cats (or rather, for their hopelessly lonely owners) but now it seemed to her justified.

An almost comically soft-spoken man (in appropriate dark suit) in the main building directed her to Sweet William's as yet unmarked grave (the stone, Lou told her, had been ordered with the inscription "Sweet William, companion and friend").

As she walked alone toward Section D, Row 14, Site 12 (a supermarket of dead things), it occurred to her that Sweet William would have liked this place; he would have raced up and down its paths, returning to her salivating and out of breath, only to race away again, looking back at her, daring her to try to catch him. She imagined him galloping at full speed away from her, turning abruptly when he heard her call, jumping up on her with dirty paws, his ears down as she chastised him, his head leaning forward for the kiss of forgiveness.

About thirty yards from her a couple stood by their pet's grave, smiling down at the newly placed flowers, the woman bending down briefly to snatch a weed that marred her surrogate baby's resting place.

Susan felt humiliated to be in their company—to witness the emptiness of their lives, to be seen displaying her own.

She found Section D and walked along its numbered rows.

"Goddamn it, Sweet William!" She saw herself, years before, in her first apartment. In her hand was a shoe, or what had been a shoe before her ungainly puppy had at it. "You're gonna get it!" It was a studio apartment, there was nowhere he could run, but, ears back, tail under, he scrambled under her bed and curled himself into the smallest ball beneath it.

"Get out of there and take what's coming to you." She was on her hands and knees, brandishing the ruined shoe at him.

He looked back at her, immense brown eyes filled with regret. If he had been human, he would have wept.

"Come on, get out of there." She tried to reach under to get him; he was too far away. "The longer you wait, the worse it'll be!"

He fell over on his side under the bed and lifted a front paw, pleading forgiveness.

"You're a rotten dog and I'm sorry I got you. . . ."

He poked the paw at the air in her direction, the eyes, even in the dark under the bed, gleaming with impossible tears.

"You pee all over the place and eat the only decent shoes I've got . . ."

He whined.

"Miserable mutt . . ."

And again.

"Rotten, cute mutt . . ."

The paw reached out to her, he laid his head on the floor, a remorseful supplicant; he whined softly, as if regretting his foolishness, his weakness, his sinfulness.

"All right, come out." Her voice was softer, though it still had an edge of anger to it.

He whined loudly now, as if praying to God to intercede.

Despite herself, Susan laughed. "Get out here, you nut."

He crawled to her, head, still too large for his young body, still on the floor, eyes, soulful, tortured eyes, not daring to look at her.

It was then that he leaned forward to be kissed, for the first time.

"Oh, lord," she had said, taking him in her arms, "what have I got myself into?"

The reverie over, Susan found herself weeping softly at Sweet William's graveside, wishing she could kiss him once more.

It was after two when she returned to the apartment. As she closed the front door, as if on cue the phones rang.

Once.

Susan stared in the direction of the kitchen (the nearest phone to her) waiting for the silence that would mean Harriet was trying to reach her.

It came.

And then the second call started. She let it ring several times (slowly entering the kitchen, still frightened at the thought of touching it), but then, remembering how sure Harriet was of herself and the world around her, she answered.

"Harriet?" she said, not yet holding the thing to her ear.

"*Fuck Harriet,*" was all she heard before slamming the receiver down.

If it was a voice that had said it, it was unlike any human voice. Surrounded by the imploded silence, it could only have been one person.

Or one thing.

"I can't describe it!" Susan said, still shivering, though Harriet had sent her secretary off to bring her a cup of coffee. (She had run from the apartment, stolen a taxi from a man who, on seeing her, was too frightened to resist, and gone directly to the phone company offices on Forty-second Street. The receptionist had immediately sent for Harriet, urgently summoning her from a meeting.)

"I don't even know if it *was* a voice," Susan said, breathing deeply, trying to slow the rush of words that were pouring out of her. "It was more like an animal's growl . . . I don't know. . . ."

"Could it have been electronic?"

"What?"

"Someone speaking through a machine?"

"I don't know. God, Harriet, I've never been so frightened . . ."

"I know, honey. Try to calm down."

"It knows about you! It knows how you'll call me!"

Harriet wanted to answer that, to assure Susan it wasn't so, but there was nothing she could say except "Try to calm down."

In a few minutes Susan did calm sufficiently for Harriet to demand, "Look, one thing you've got to do. No matter how scared you are, the next time it calls, you mustn't hang up. Put the phone down, get out of the apartment, come here if you like, but don't hang up. We can't do a thing if you hang up."

"I understand," Susan replied, ashamed of her inability to assist the only person who might help her. "I won't. I promise."

"Good girl." And with a glance at her wristwatch, "Shit, it's three-fifteen. I've got a roomful of minor executives out there waiting to snipe at me. Gotta go. Walk you to the elevator."

They walked to the elevator bank together, Harriet assuring her that something would be done about her caller, that sooner or later, he (it?) would be caught and put where he belonged.

"He's just some creep, Susan. Every once in a while one of them crawls out of the woodwork. You can't let him get to you."

Thoroughly ashamed, Susan nodded and watched Harriet as she hurried off to her meeting, feeling that if this horror were happening to her, she would know how to deal with it; she had everything Susan lacked, including courage.

She was halfway to the lobby when she remembered Andrea, alone after school, waiting for her.

One more shame.

Their chance came.

It was early the next morning. Susan could still hear the closing door of the elevator that was taking Lou and Andrea off for the day.

One ring. Silence. The second call.

She stood in the kitchen, still holding her coffee cup, aware that she was beginning to tremble, knowing it wasn't Harriet (she wouldn't be at her office yet; she wouldn't call from home), certain that the thing waited on the other end of the line, waited to laugh at her or worse.

Harriet's words came back to her ("Don't hang up!") and she silently gave her promise once more.

She approached the phone, hesitated, felt Harriet's imagined impatience with her and picked it up.

As she held it to her ear, she heard Harriet's voice.

"Look, one thing you've got to do. No matter how scared you are, the next time it calls, you mustn't hang up. Put the phone down, get out of the apartment, come here if you like . . ."

"Harriet?" she said.

". . . but don't hang up. We can't do a thing if you hang up."

"Harriet, what are you saying?"

"I understand. I won't. I promise."

Susan recognized her own voice.

"Good girl . . ."

"Harriet? Harriet?" she called out as if she could reach through what they had said to the Harriet who now existed.

". . . *Shit, it's three-fifteen. I've got a roomful of* . . ."

"Stop it!"

". . . *out there waiting to snipe at me. Gotta go* . . ."

"Damn you! I won't hang up!"

". . . *walk you to the elevator* . . ."

"You won't make me hang up this time!"

". . . *so, how do you like our offices? Snazzy, huh?* . . ."

Susan slammed the receiver down on the kitchen counter with such force that the earpiece split, sending a semicircle of white plastic skittering to the floor, where it trembled for a moment and came to rest at her feet. She stared down at it as if it were a dismembered human part.

In a moment she became aware that no sound came from the remaining, shattered part.

She hurried to the living room and pulled the second receiver from its cradle.

Only the sound of a dial tone.

Cursing her stupidity, Susan vowed that the next time she was called, no trick, no obscene joke, no matter how unexpected, would make her fail in her promise.

Susan smelled smoke.

It haunted her that entire evening as she searched for the source. (Lou smelled nothing and grew annoyed with her constant opening and slamming of doors and cupboards.) But the smell persisted. (Three times she checked the service area and the outer hallway; she opened and shut the oven door a dozen times; she checked lamp wires and the two TV

sets, even the transistor radio she had brought back
from the office.)

And still the acrid odor of fire persisted.

And in her sole dream that night.

She saw Harriet as a doll ("A regular doll," Tara's
voice giggled somewhere in the darkness of the
dream). But the doll was burning. Harriet was burning, her mane of hair frizzing from the heat and then
exploding into flames. Her face, each lovely feature,
melting, discoloring, flowing off the head into puddles beside it. Her dress (the one she'd worn to lunch)
turning brown, black, incinerating.

Susan woke (late as always, alone in the apartment) knowing the truth, and for the first time in
weeks she voluntarily reached for her bedside phone.

"Harriet?" she said, when she reached her. "It's
Susan."

There was a hesitation. "You're using the phone,"
Harriet said.

"Yes, I had to. Are you all right?" And her voice
pleaded that she was.

"Sure. What's the matter?"

Susan doubted for a moment, felt foolish but
pushed the question.

"Nothing happened last night?"

"What?"

"Did anything happen? Was there a fire?"

Another hesitation in which Susan heard the
answer. And then, "How the hell did you know
that?"

It was as she'd surmised—a warning; fire from a
world of fire.

"What happened?" Susan asked, sickened.

"It was the oven. Larry thought I turned it down and I thought he did. But how did you know?"

"I smelled it."

"What?"

"Harriet, I want you to listen to me and to do exactly what I tell you—" and the image of a hand (her hand) releasing a lifeline came to Susan. "I want you to stop tracing my calls. I want you to forget you ever met me. . . ."

"Susan, what on earth are you talking about?"

"I don't want your help. I want you to leave me alone." And she thought of Jimmy and Sweet William.

"Why? What have I done?"

"It's not what you've done, Harriet. It's what's going to happen to you if you don't leave me alone! Please, for your own sake . . ."

"Susan, come on, calm down . . ."

"There's nothing you can do. Don't you see that?" She forced a calm, better to protect her friend. "The fire was a warning, Harriet. It knows you're trying to help me. It won't let you . . ."

"Susan, that's ridiculous. It was just a small fire in the oven. We have mishaps like that all the time. I mean, if there's a worse slob in this world than Larry, it's me. . . ."

"Please, Harriet, *please*!"

"Susan, we're practically there. When I got into the office there was a call from the guys in computer readout. Yesterday they registered a call on your line, but you hung up too fast. . . ."

"It won't make any difference. I don't want you harmed."

"I'm not going to be."

"Please, Harriet, please . . ." she begged weakly.

"Look—" Harriet's voice came back at her filled with a sudden authority. "This isn't just a favor, Susan. I'm part of the phone company and we don't like our instruments used to torment people. Honey," she softened, "face it. Like it or not, I'm on your side."

"Forgive me," Susan said after a pause in which she realized it was useless to plead any more. "Forgive me for getting you involved."

"Don't be silly."

"You're a wonderful person. . . ." She was crying.

"You, too. We're all wonderful people with one glaring exception. And we'll get him, Susan. I promise you, okay?"

"Okay."

"And when we do, you owe me dinner at the Palace, is it a deal?"

"Yes."

"You know the cheapest bottle of wine there is seventy-five bucks? I want you to know what you're getting yourself into."

"You've got it," Susan sniffled into the phone, smiling.

"And I'm a hell of a wine drinker."

"You're a hell of a woman."

"We aim to please. Now stop crying and go out to a movie. That's what I always do."

"I will. Thank you."

"See you at the Palace." And she hung up.

Susan replaced the receiver and rolled over in bed. Finding herself on Lou's side (unfamiliar, seeing the room from his eyes), she thought of Florence and the Arno.

The phone rang.

She thought of Harriet, blessed Harriet, as she picked it up.

It was there, waiting for her, as she knew it would be.

She placed the receiver down on the bed gently (her teeth were chattering, her lips trembling) and left the room.

In Andrea's bed (the door closed) she could hear nothing. She lay there wondering how she could ever express her gratitude to Harriet. Her awe. Her love.

She would never get the chance.

Harriet sat at her desk, looking at the phone she had just hung up.

"Poor baby," she muttered to herself as her intercom buzzed.

"Uh-huh?" she said into it.

"It's Tony from the twenty-second floor. On Three."

She pressed into his call.

"Miss Walgreen, there's something wild going on on the Reed line, the one you asked us to monitor. You wanna see it?"

"I'll be right up." She headed for the door. "We've got you, you bastard," and her secretary, overhearing her, wondered who was in trouble now.

Harriet stepped out of the elevator on twenty-two, smiled, thinking of the only time she had ever eaten at the Palace (the bill, lunch for four of them, came to over three hundred dollars) and walked down the hall to the switching network. She pressed the correct combination of numbers on its door safe and pushed the heavy metal door open.

Inside, the usual sound of millions of separate clicks combined into one low static welcomed her. She always enjoyed the sound, authoritarian and important—a long way from Brooklyn.

She walked between two rows of computer banks, ten feet tall, eighty feet long, filled with thousands of terminals. "The largest corporation in the world," she often told friends proudly.

"Hi, Tony," she said, reaching his office, cubbyholed behind the gargantuan machines. "What's up?"

"You tell me." He held out a readout sheet to her.

Harriet took it, saw the endless lists of pale-blue numbers that meant nothing to her. "I'll wait till they make the movie."

"Look—" he picked up a pencil and hurriedly circled Susan's number—"here's the Reed number, the one the tap is on." He circled it four times, twice at the top of the list, once in the middle, once at the bottom. "According to this, the call is coming from trunk line 01603."

"Uh-huh," Harriet said, aware that Tony was bristling. "So?"

"So, that's Santa Monica."

"Great."

"Not so great. I called the tandem office there and they have no readout on any calls to the Reed number. . . ."

Harriet felt a chill, a slight one, and buttoned her jacket.

". . . Moreover, that trunk line is down. 01603 hasn't been used in two days. So where the hell are the calls coming from?"

"That's impossible."

"You bet it is . . . unless . . ." He shook his head.

"Unless what?"

"Unless somebody's beaming into our satellite system. How important is this Reed guy?"

Another man stepped forward from the corner of the room, frightening Harriet, who hadn't noticed him sitting there. "Or unless the caller's got his own microwave tower. Listen, for a couple of million dollars, I could call, too, and you wouldn't find me."

Tony, on the verge of anger (he had traced kidnappers and spies in his twenty years with the company), waved him away.

"Come with me, Miss Walgreen. I'll show it to you on the output terminal. It's coming in, regular as clockwork."

Harriet (definitely chilled now, wishing she had worn the sweater she always kept behind the door of her office) followed Tony into the switching room. They passed the computer banks (tens of thousands of terminals, hundreds of thousands of resistors, all the size of miniature bullets), and went to the small machine dwarfed by the others, the "stars" of the system.

They stood before it and watched the TV screen as numbers flashed on.

All the while, the low static of clicks.

"See?" Tony pointed to the screen. "Here it is again."

"Damn it," Harriet muttered.

And the sound of the clicking grew more intense.

"Listen, Miss Walgreen, is there something about this you haven't told me?"

"Like what?"

"I don't know. Is it a test of some kind? Some new jamming equipment?"

"Tony, what would I have to do with that?"

And louder.

"Listen to this," someone across the room said to a coworker.

"I don't know," Tony replied sheepishly. "There's just something not kosher going on."

"Jesus . . ."

"It's not a joke or a test, Tony."

"Why's it doing that?"

"I don't know."

Now the static, three, four times louder than normal, interrupted them.

"Hey, Pat, what's going on?" Tony called to a man far down a row of computers.

"Your guess is as good as mine."

"It sounds like a swarm of locusts got in here," another offered.

And the sound swelled.

"Holy Christ!" someone said.

The machines started to tremble. All of them.

"What's going on?"

"It sounds like an earthquake."

"What the hell . . ."

"Look at this," one technician said to another, pointing at a row of terminals that vibrated, adding the sound of clapping metal to the machine-gunning clicks.

And the resistors, by the hundreds of thousands, shook wildly within the terminals.

"Holy Christ . . ."

"What's going on? . . ."

"Call upstairs, will you? . . ."

Suddenly, in one giant shatter, the resistors exploded out of the terminals, each one a small, lethal piece of shrapnel.

Aimed at Harriet.

Their impact was simultaneous.

She fell, like red snow.

18

It was a half hour before Susan dared enter her bedroom.

It was filled with it.

She ran to her closet, trying not to listen, not to succumb, but it was useless. Her hands shook so violently she could barely remove the clothes she would need to escape the apartment.

She slammed the bedroom door behind her and dressed in the kitchen (two closed doors between her and it), but the knowledge that it was there, that it was filling one room and might spill out into the hallway, prevented her from calming herself and the dressing took time.

She thought she heard it as the elevator doors closed but she couldn't be sure; her head was trembling, she might have imagined it.

On the corner of West End Avenue and Seventy- .

seventh Street the pay phone had been repaired. She lifted its receiver.

It was there.

She hailed a cab and went to Harriet.

There was an ambulance in front of the building as she arrived. And a red van pulling away.

"My God," Tara said softly. She had said it many times since Susan burst into her office and told her it had killed Harriet. "My God."

She believed, at last.

They planned. Though she hated the idea and feared it, Susan would have to go away, alone— to remove herself (and it) from Andrea and Lou. (Though Tara said nothing, she silently added her name to the list.) Then they, at least, would be safe.

"You're one gutsy lady," Tara said, reaching for her hand.

It was decided she would go to Tara's parents' country house, two hours up the thruway.

"Maybe it won't find you there," Tara said, expecting no response and getting none.

They called Olin's and reserved a car for Susan. Tara drew a map to the house ("My God," she still muttered) and they prepared to leave the office. Tara would go to her parents' apartment and get the keys to the house, then pick up Andrea at school. Susan would hire the car, go to the apartment (the phones had to be dealt with) and pack.

As they entered the reception area, Maudey was there.

"Susan, dear, how are you?" She extended a perfectly manicured hand. "Off for the day, Tara?" And an I-dare-you smile flashed across her face.

"Off for the day, Commissar Ninotchka," Tara answered, guiding Susan to the door.

*   *   *

The car parked downstairs, Susan entered the apartment. She went into the kitchen for the shears (the white phone, still dead, watched her in silent anger) and quickly sliced through its cord.

The same in the living room.

Then to the real test, the live phone in the bedroom.

As she walked slowly down the hallway, the Silence, still there, grew thicker and more oppressive. She found herself perspiring, starting to tremble (as always), and she held tight to the comforting hardness of the shears.

It was done quickly, but not before a wave of nausea washed over her that nearly caused her to vomit. The power of the thing, if anything, was increasing.

She packed quickly and sat in the living room to await Andrea.

Andrea, whom she would not see for . . . but it did no good to think of it and so she dismissed it from her mind. Tara would make the arrangements. Her mother, after school, Lou, evenings and weekends.

Lou.

No, she decided. She wouldn't face him yet. Later, when she returned. For now, Tara would explain it to him (would *try* to explain it to him; even Harriet's death might not penetrate his arrogant defenses).

At three-thirty, Tara and Andrea arrived.

"But where are you going?" Andrea, petulant at the news, scowled at her.

"Sweetheart, it's business. A little business trip, that's all. I'll be back in a week . . . or two. . . ."

"Do you have to go?"

"Yes, I'm afraid I do." And she took her in her arms, glancing helplessly over the child's shoulder to Tara.

"I don't want you to go."

"I know, darling, but I have to. You'll have Daddy and Grammy to take care of you. . . ."

"Want to go to the circus with me, honey?" Tara tried to help.

Andrea held fast to her mother, resisting the offer. "I don't want you to go."

"I love you, darling. I love you so much."

"If you love me, don't go."

"I have to, sweetheart. I have to."

Hours later, on the highway, the scene returned to Susan and for a moment she had difficulty seeing the road.

She left the thruway at New Paltz and drove through the small college town looking for Route 32. The sun, low on the horizon, bathed the one- and two-story buildings in a pale yellow-white light (a light hardly ever seen in Manhattan, where the larger buildings blocked it out, forcing evening), and she felt as if she were in a completely alien landscape. But a beautiful one, she acknowledged, finding Route 32 and starting north again. She vaguely remembered Ulster County from her childhood (summer camp, a weekend with her parents at Mohonk Manor) but had forgotten its special charm. It was a down-at-the heels area with none of the pretensions of Connecticut or Westchester. There were farms, honest-to-God farms, dotting the rolling hills, and white stone houses that dated back to the eighteenth century, all interspersed with modest split-levels and tacky Victorians. It seemed to her the area had been frozen, timeless, since she was a child, and that feeling comforted her.

She crossed a covered bridge over a pond. The sky was streaked now with arrowlike clouds and there was a gold glow on the horizon, giving way to the palest blue-green she had ever seen. Susan ached at that moment to be an artist again. To be anything again, rather than what she was: a displaced person, running uselessly from what could not be escaped.

Or could it? There, in the midst of grandeur (the grandeur that was the only possible proof of God), she was not so sure.

She turned west at Rifton (Tara had spelled it wrong on the map: Riftone) and followed the winding road down its course beside a river (exquisite, untouched), a series of stone buildings (Norman Rockwell had not made it up, after all) and the thickness of woods (real woods, not the simulated miniature patches she was used to).

She rolled down the window and inhaled the fragrance of leaves and decay and new growth.

If anywhere was to be safe, surely it was here. Perhaps, if so, she could send for Andrea. Perhaps the nightmare had an end.

The house sat back in the woods on a cliff over the river. It was three stories high, a stone hunting lodge, a fantasy house from movies she had seen as a child (Cary Grant, coming down the staircase, framed in hand-hewn beams, Irene Dunne at the fireplace, hopeless at lighting a fire). She had no idea Tara *came from money*. The living room was on the second floor, cathedral ceiling, with two small bedrooms upstairs on an open balcony. There was a covered terrace, arched stone walls, overlooking the river and the hill beyond. The view reminded her of Switzerland: spruce and pine and other evergreens as far up and down the river as she could see; not another house, no signs of civilization . . . except . . . Susan shuddered at the sight of the electrical lines crossing the river far upstream. Telephone lines.

She went back inside and searched for the phones. One in the small bedroom on the balcony; another in the living room, on the piano.

She went downstairs, through a Mediterranean sitting-dining room (completely at odds with the rest of the house) into its kitchen. A third phone, on the wall next to the refrigerator (just as in her apartment —kitchen, living room, bedroom).

She contemplated cutting them but rejected the thought for the moment, being a guest in a stranger's home. Nonetheless, she searched the room's drawers until she found a pair of scissors and left them out.

Then, darkness descending rapidly, she turned on lights, brought wood in from the terrace and made a fire. (Unlike Irene, Susan was adept at it.) She settled in a beige chaise beside the fire, looked around at the soft country elegance of the room and, as if the house itself would protect her, closed her eyes and was asleep.

She was wakened by the ringing of the phones.

Opening her eyes, finding herself in a strange place (it took a moment to recall where she was and why), Susan lay there, refusing to answer, staring at the glowing embers in the fireplace, feeling cold.

She did answer, eventually.

"Susan, what the hell is going on?" It was Lou, calling from the apartment.

"Didn't Tara tell you?"

"She told me a lot of crap, that's what she told me."

"It isn't *crap*, Lou. Harriet thought it was crap and now she's dead."

"Jesus, Susan, what's the matter with you?" And they argued.

To no avail. At Lou's insistence that she come home ("I've had it, Susan! Enough already!") she stonily refused. In the end, she promised to consider it and to call (if it was safe). Lou would come up on the weekend; again, if it was safe.

She went downstairs and searched the refrigerator. It was empty.

Thus, having nothing to eat and not knowing where a restaurant or store might be (afraid to attempt finding one in the dark), Susan went upstairs to the large bedroom (the one without a phone) and miserably went to bed.

And a quarter of a mile upstream, a beaver woke from its sleep and hurried to the telephone pole near the river. With frenzied eyes, against its will, it started to chew.

Susan woke late to find the house even lovelier in sunshine than it was by firelight. She had hardly noticed the bric-a-brac the night before, but now, coffee in hand (there was coffee, a small blessing), she wandered through its rooms, examining it. There was a small collection of wooden and pottery ducks, a turn-of-the-century black boy with a fishing pole and a large simpleton's smile (the bigoted fashion of the day), framed silhouettes and flowers. Charming, all.

She played "Für Elise" on the piano (hopelessly out of tune) and again grew aware that she was hungry.

She drove back to Route 32, turned north toward Rosendale (Rosendale cement occurred to her, a bit of trivia from her past) and found a roadside diner.

The sign over the counter read "Special Breakfast: Two eggs, orange juice, coffee, toast, potatoes. $1.35." The area was definitely frozen in time.

Having finished her meal and listened to the loud cheery voices of the regulars ("You planting roses this summer, Rico?" "Nah, too much trouble, too much trouble." "What's trouble? Plant climbers." "Yeah, maybe climbers"), Susan left, got back in the car and decided to drive through the area.

She found herself in High Falls, a one-street hamlet straight off a turn-of-the-century postcard. She parked the car in front of the Egg's Nest (a pub, here in the middle of the woods, a wonder) and strolled across the road to its two antique shops. In one of them she found a star-covered quilt and stood before it, remembering another time.

"Lou, if we don't buy it, it'll haunt us the rest of our lives." They were younger then, in their twenties, as yet childless.

"Two hundred dollars? For a rocking chair?"

"Would you pay two hundred dollars for President Kennedy's rocking chair?"

"If he was in it."

"Let me put it to you this way. Either we buy it or I'll kill you."

"How?" and he cupped her behind in his hand. "You wanna fuck me to death?"

"Stop."

"Nobody's looking."

"Stop." She pushed his hand away.

"I'll make you a deal," he said, moving the displaced hand to her waist. "I'll buy it if you come back to the hotel with me."

"Now?"

"Yeah."

"We just did it."

"I wanna do it again till we get it right."

"You creep." She laughed. "You'll really buy it?"

"You'll really come back to the hotel?"

"No deals, just buy it." And she summoned the proprietor.

As Lou struggled to wedge the chair into the back seat of their car, Susan said, "Hurry up. We have to go back to the hotel."

She woke from the reverie as a cat, large and red, pushed the length of its body against her leg. She ran her hand over it, saw its shedding hair fly off, and walked on.

She drove through farmland all afternoon, down roads busy with housewives, scratching at their gardens in preparation for the spring show, past rivers and waterfalls, Wyeth barns, white stucco taverns, trees that seemed centuries old, a field of grazing cows (which looked up at her en masse).

She returned to the house at four in the afternoon, peaceful, joyous, purged.

At five, after a short nap, she woke, yearning to walk in the woods. Dressing for it (it had never occurred to her to bring proper shoes—never mind), she knew that if they lived here, away from the city, they would be safe.

She thought briefly of how to convince Lou and fought a momentary depression caused by the hopelessness of trying.

The woods (across the circular driveway, behind the unexpected barn) were everything she hoped they'd be: silent, untouched, brown with dead leaves (a carpet, she thought, smiling at the cliché), the trees just starting to renew themselves. She heard the shrill scream of two blue jays berating each other, high above. The ferns were coming up quickly, uncoiling small tentacles of lush green. It was so lovely she wished she could cry from the beauty of it, but of course, she could not. No one ever could.

She climbed a small precipice and, standing on its peak, saw the river and the woods on the other side.

And then, motion.

A terrible shattering of the silence as something across the river, on its steep wooded slope, ran, crashing among the trees.

It shivered the branches as it descended to the river.

Susan, taken unawares, frightened, saw a doe running, slipping down the embankment. It seemed to be having a fit, legs kicking, trying to right itself, losing the battle.

It plunged into the river as she watched, horrified. And then, struggling with its deformed legs, it crawled out of the water and lay on its side on the rocky shore, panting, emitting a low rasping sound.

She had never seen a wild animal die, and it shocked her; the unreasonableness of it seemed unnatural. Nature's death should be swift or calm—not like this.

The doe raised its head, arched its neck and turned, looking straight across the river at Susan.

She saw its red eyes, its tongue protruding, the nostrils pumping air.

And on its face, even that distance away, she recognized Sweet William in the closet, driven mad while he waited for her.

And she knew she had brought her obscenity with her.

19

It waited for the men to repair the line (the beaver was found dead next to the fallen pole, dead birds nearby) and then gleefully attacked.

Susan was sleeping heavily, having found the Karsian liquor cabinet. She dreamed, as she always did of late, dreams of dread and loss, of her father angry, and her mother taking his side or no side, never Susan's.

As the dream lightened (Tara came into it), it called.

She woke slowly to the ringing, five or six glasses of sweet wine between her and it, and lay there, fully awake, listening to it.

She rose, put on Tara's mother's robe (she had brought nothing heavy enough for the still cold country evenings) and went to it.

She expected she could deal with it (an old enemy, familiar by now) better than she had in the past; she knew what to expect—she could always hang up, her sole power.

She was wrong.

Its intensity, if anything, was stronger (the ungodly Silence inside the house; the alien country silence outside).

When Susan hung up (quickly as always) she was shivering, pulling the robe tight around her, hearing her own teeth chatter.

She went downstairs and lit a fire. Sitting on the hearth, feeling the warmth, drinking gin (sweet wine would not do, not now), she realized that all this (the Silence, the deaths, the torment) was merely a preamble.

Soon, it would tell her what it wanted.

Soon, it would call her.

To hell.

She saw in her mind the artist's hell of special effects in the movie Andrea had been watching. She remembered her own childhood version: it was a building, an enormous government building whose main hallway resembled Grand Central Station (her mother had taken her there one afternoon, to meet an incoming friend). Under a mighty rotunda, people came and went to their private damnations. There were no flames, no cries of agony, no pleading for mercy. Just a remorseful resignation as the people (a silent army, unlike the angry one of the slums of New York) came and went, eternally en route from one pain to another, loveless, hopeless, living out a sadness that had no end.

Was it, she wondered, that much different from life? (She remembered Andrea and decided that it was; no matter what else she had lived through, failures, the loss of Lou, there was still Andrea, precious and perfect, to make it all worthwhile.)

She ached, briefly, for her daughter, ached to hold and stroke her, and then returned to bed and the dreams that nightly prevented any true rest.

And as she slept, it devised a new torture.

Ninety miles away, in Greenwich Village, a phone rang, and Tara, herself asleep next to Yuri (a temporary reunion), answered it.

Susan pondered over coffee early the next afternoon (she wakened after twelve) and decided: she took up the scissors and with difficulty (her hands seemed weak to her) cut through the kitchen-phone cord. She also severed the other phones (cutting the bedroom cord in three pieces as well as the receiver cord). Then she returned to the kitchen, finished her coffee and dressed.

The afternoon was gray (sky and hills blending into one another, gray to gray) as she drove. The same relentless sadness that now filled her days seemed to have settled over the land: regret everywhere, even in the trees whose gnarled branches seemed to be held up against the sky, rather than toward it.

She lunched at a small roadside restaurant, nearly empty (one elderly woman in the corner ate and read voraciously) and decorated in the manner of a country kitchen. Copper pots and pans, calico animals, pottery vases and urns. At another time it would have been charming; now Susan saw only the hints of squalor (a broken windowpane, a badly repaired hutch along its main wall).

She returned to the car and drove south on Route 209, searching either side of the road for some diversion.

It came just outside Accord—a large plant nursery

with four enormous greenhouses. (Had she ever been to a nursery before? she wondered, and decided she hadn't.) She pulled the car into its parking lot and entered the first greenhouse.

It was impressively large, perhaps a hundred feet deep, and was divided into three rows of plants, two aisles between them. The central row, the widest, was filled with coleus plants by the hundreds, each five or six inches tall, each in its own small clay pot. She recalled the coleus of her youth that sat in her mother's kitchen, refusing, year after year, to die. It became long and straggly, and its course of growth toward the sun made it ramble all over the window. (Eventually her mother had tired of seeing it and she threw it away, but its shadow still adhered to the glass and sill, small bits of it, shreds of stem and branch long cemented there.)

Behind the coleus was a mass of Caladiums, cheerful even on this gloomy day. Their colors, pink, green, purple, had always amused her and now were a welcome relief from the mournful memory of her mother's coleus. (Why had she thrown it away? Would she throw her away, too?)

Susan caressed one of the oversized leaves; she had never realized her fondness for plants, but now, in this dreadful state, the Caladiums seemed a small voice of friendliness.

She decided to buy one, and as she searched among them (which to choose—the hardy deep green or the translucent pink-and-white?) she heard a phone ring, far off. (*It has nothing to do with me*, she thought.)

There was one with three leaves, two pink and one green. She removed it from the tightly packed field of pots.

(*Everyone in the world gets phone calls. It has nothing to do with me.*)

Then, thinking better of it, she replaced it and chose another, larger plant.

(Answer it, why don't you?)

The ringing stopped and Susan retraced her steps and removed the first plant; she would buy them both. (Had she actually felt a tinge of guilt over returning it? Did her mother feel the same when their coleus, long a member of the family, had been carted away beyond recall with the rest of the refuse?)

She saw the back door of the greenhouse and exited, carrying both plants.

The next greenhouse, the arrowed sign announced, held early lilies. Susan walked between packing crates and shelves of rooted cuttings to its rear door. On entering, she smiled widely at the sight of thousands of white lilies, haphazardly arranged on three tiers, the large ornate blossoms pointing in each and every direction.

And in the corner, as yet unseen, the telephone, its receiver off the hook.

Susan strolled down the aisle, noticed the lack of scent (beauty *and* scent would be too much) and decided to buy several. She found a plastic carrying tray along the wall and placed her two Caladiums in it.

She chose two lily plants, four blossoms each, and one with several unopened buds. And then she turned and saw:

A semicircle of dead lilies, brown, dried and shriveled.

All in the corner by the phone.

She fled.

That evening after dinner (a little food; much Karsian gin) Susan sat outside on the terrace, a quilt bundled about her, watching the dwindling daylight turn the water of the river lavender. The sky was immense; living in the city, she hardly saw it. What, she wondered, can this alienation from nature do to one? Can it make you crazy?

Was that the answer? As simple as that?

She wished she were crazy; she begged silently for it. To be crazy had an end, no matter how grim. But this, this nightmare, threatened to go on until it became another reality, somewhere else, somewhere that had always existed and always would.

She pulled the quilt tight around her.

A shaft of yellow light cut across the terrace. She looked up, concerned but not yet frightened, and saw a car pulling into the driveway.

In a moment, she and Tara stood facing each other across the front threshold.

"Oh, honey," Susan said, reaching for her, burying her face in the warmth between Tara's neck and shoulder. "I'm so glad you came."

They went to the fireplace, sat in front of it, saw each other in the glow of the fire.

"What's the matter?" Susan asked, seeing the pain in Tara's eyes.

Tara looked away, hiding it.

"What is it?"

"You have to go," Tara said, still not looking at her. "You have to go."

"Go? Where?"

"Away from here." The words came slowly and with enormous difficulty. Tara took her hand and held it tightly. "You have to leave the house."

"Why?"

Now Tara did look at her, and Susan saw the mixture of shame and fear that told her what she needed to know. "It called you."

"Yes."

"You heard it?"

"Yes." And Tara started to cry.

Susan took her in her arms. "Don't. Shhh . . ."

"I'm frightened, Susan. I'm so frightened. . . ."

"I know, baby, I know. . . ."

"I keep thinking of Harriet!"

"Shhh . . ."

"I'm sorry, Susan. I wish I was braver but I'm so frightened. . . ."

"I know, I know. Don't cry." She stroked her friend.

"It knows you're here and that I'm helping you. Otherwise, it wouldn't have called me. God, Susan, when I hung up the phone I was sick! Literally sick!"

"I know."

"I vomited all over myself!"

"Shhh . . ."

"Please don't hate me, Susan. Please."

"I don't hate you. I love you."

"But I'm throwing you out. . . ."

"No, you're not. You're doing what you have to do, I understand that. I wouldn't have come here if I thought it would find out."

"It did. It knows everything!"

Susan left the fireplace and poured Tara a glass of white wine. (The bottle was almost empty; she should replace it before going.)

Tara drank quickly, calming, reaching for Susan's hand, which she kissed.

"Why *you*, Susan? Why does it want *you*?"

"I don't know."

"Did you ever do anything . . . ?" She groped for an appropriate word.

"No, I don't think I did." They were silent for a

moment and then Susan added, "Maybe there isn't a reason. Maybe we're just chosen at random."

"What are you going to do?"

"I don't know."

"God, Susan, I don't want you to go." Tara looked as though she might cry again.

"I know, sweetheart, I know—" and she stroked her cheek. "But there's nothing we can do about it."

"I'm frightened," Tara repeated.

"I'll go tonight."

"No, don't!" and Tara's shame was there again. "Tomorrow. Sleep tonight."

"All right. Thank you." Susan forced a smile of gratitude. "We'll have a last pajama party."

Tara looked into the fire, discomforted.

"No," Susan said. "Of course you can't stay."

"I want to."

"No, you go back to town. I'll be all right." The idiocy of what she was saying made her chuckle. "*You'll* be all right."

Tara got up, as if she had been waiting for Susan's permission, and hugged her.

"I'm sorry about the phones," Susan said, recalling that she had cut the wires.

"What?"

Susan glanced over at the phone on the piano. She traced its cord to the wall.

Intact.

"Nothing, never mind," she said, turning Tara toward the door and walking with her, to make it easier. "Do me a favor?"

"Of course," and she added, "if I can."

"See Andrea when you get back to town. Remember, you promised to take her to the circus."

Tara turned at the door, crying again. "I'll take

care of her," she said, and quickly hugged her friend. "I love you."

"I love you, too."

Then Tara hurried out of the house, across the lawn and to her car.

Susan watched as the small Volvo sped out of the driveway to safety. Se returned to the fire and slowly finished Tara's glass of wine.

Had Tara thought more carefully about it, she would have realized that the thing could not let her live, now that she knew of its existence.

The thought did occur to her (half-formed) as she pulled onto the thruway at New Paltz and headed south.

Hardly a minute went by before a red van, heading north, went out of control, jumped the barrier and destroyed the Volvo.

And her along with it.

20

The Rhinecliff Bridge spanned the Hudson at a particularly wide spot. Driving across it, midmorning the next day, Susan glanced down and saw the river, still unspoiled, and the mansions that dotted its shores, their tended velvet lawns that sloped down to the water, their porticos and elegant columns.

"Doric, Ionic, Corinthian," she said aloud, refusing to think, forbidding it, rejecting it completely.

(If these were her last days on earth, she would no longer waste them on fighting back. She would take away with her what she could—the memory of beauty and love. She would gather them as luggage, the only luggage possible.)

She drove the better part of the day, choosing back roads that would bring her closer to the lives she wished to see.

The old people (the lucky ones) whose children had

grown up before their eyes and whose grandchildren now grew; and the middle-aged ones settled into comfort; and, of course, the children.

She stopped the car on the main street of one small town to watch the children. When the ache became too sharp, she drove on, joining Andrea, in her mind, at her drawing board.

As dusk settled over the country, she found a small motel (she was vaguely on the way to Albany) and registered.

"Mrs. Reed? Oh, yes." The clerk, a portly man in his sixties who had glanced down at her signature through thick bifocals, turned to a stack of papers beside him. "Just got a message for you. Maybe a minute ago."

"For me?"

"Mrs. *Susan* Reed?"

"Yes."

He handed her the paper.

Call Harriet Walgreen. 212-733-4020.

"Room 214. Here's your key. Mrs. Reed? . . . You hear me, Mrs. Reed?"

Susan looked up from the paper into the thickness of his lenses, her own vision blurred at that moment as her eyes filled with tears.

"You all right, Mrs. Reed?" He extended the key.

"No—I've changed my mind," she said, turning and walking away quickly.

He snorted and as she pushed through the front door she heard him mutter, "This isn't an answering service, ya'know."

She drove for another forty-five minutes, north, knowing it was watching her. It had called as she pulled into the motel; it would call again, no matter where she went.

Of course she was right.

At the second motel (larger, part of a renowned chain) the clerk (younger, robust) handed her the message.

Call Harriet Walgreen. Urgent. 212-733-4020.

She allowed the clerk to hand her a key and went to the room. There, sitting on one of its double-size twin beds, she stared at the phone, the grotesque message in her hand.

She dialed.

She listened to the ringing (it sounded as if it were coming from a distance, but an earthly one). And then—

"Susan? Honey, thank God you called." It was Harriet's voice, unmistakably.

"I've been so worried about you. I know what you must be going through. . . ."

She listened, numbly.

"But Susan, you mustn't be afraid. Please, honey, listen to me. . . ."

She hung up, breathless.

And then, like Tara, she was sick.

It didn't call her back that night and Susan slept deeply and dreamlessly for the first night in weeks.

The following morning, Susan breakfasted at a pancake house along a busy road. (Caldor, Sears, Wanamaker's, she counted the familiar names, still gathering her luggage.)

As she finished her second cup of coffee (she was pleased that they brought her a pot of her own, an unexpected nicety) the waitress—who, had she lived in the city would have been pretty but here in the country already tended to stoutness—came up to her.

"Excuse me, is your name Reed?"

The look of apprehension on Susan's face caused her to take a step backward.

"Mrs. Reed?"

"Yes," Susan answered curtly.

"There's a phone call for you."

"I'm sure there is."

"Back there." The waitress smiled, pointing.

"Tell them I'm not here." Susan returned to her coffee.

The girl hesitated. (Here in the country, where things were simple, people answered their calls obediently.)

"Tell them I just left," Susan said, not looking at her.

The girl obeyed, confused. (Later she would tell a friend about it, when it made sense to her. The city woman was waiting for a man to join her; he was calling to cancel; perhaps his wife had found out about them.)

Susan finished her coffee slowly, angrily. (How dare they use Harriet's voice against her. How dare they insult her memory!)

She overtipped the girl (none of it was her fault, she hadn't deserved Susan's rudeness) and left.

On the road again, heading nowhere, angry and wary (not frightened any more, though—that had been burned out of her), she decided to face her persecutors. She would answer the next call.

It came early that evening as Susan was shown to her room in a somewhat luxurious hotel across the Massachusetts border. (She would treat herself better from now on.)

She was sitting on a wicker settee, looking out the window at the hotel's pond, on which two ducks (wild or placed there) slowly paddled, dipping their bills occasionally into the water, when the phone rang.

She stared at it angrily, aware that she was still not frightened, not in the least—the bully had lost its power over her in that, at least.

"Susan? Please don't hang up," Harriet's voice (only her voice, not Harriet, she reminded herself) said as she held it up to her ear.

"I'm not going to," Susan replied.

"Thank God for that," Harriet said.

"You're blaspheming, dear." And Susan sat on the bed and lit a cigarette.

"What's the matter, honey? You sound mad."

"Do I?"

"Are you mad at me?"

"Why would I be mad at you?"

"I don't know."

"Don't you?"

"Susan, please, I only called to help."

"Did you?"

"Of course, why else?"

"That's true. You've always been such a help, Harriet."

"Why are you being sarcastic?"

"I'm not. You have always helped me, haven't you?"

"I've tried to."

"And you've succeeded. And now you want to help me some more, is that it, Harriet? Is that why you keep calling me?"

"Of course."

"Harriet?"

"Yes?"

"Fuck you."

There was a pause before Harriet's voice (only her voice, Susan repeated to herself, only her voice) reacted. "Why did you say that?"

"Dunno."

"Susan, I'm your friend!" And the voice feigned hurt.

"Fuck you, friend."

Another hesitation and then, "Wait a minute. Tara wants to talk to you."

Stunned, Susan waited.

"Susan?" It was Tara's voice. "What's going on?"

"Tara?" she said, for the moment believing it.

"Yeah. Harriet says you're mad at her. Why?"

"Tara, what are you saying?"

"Listen, will you just *listen*? Stop running away and listen to us. . . ."

"What?" Susan shouted into the phone.

"First of all, calm down, will you? There's nothing to be afraid of, Susan. I swear to you. I swear on my life there's nothing to be afraid of. . . ."

"What are you saying?"

"It's all so simple when you really understand it. Look, we can't talk over the phone. Come back to town and meet us. Let us talk to you."

"No," Susan said.

"Will you *listen* to me? Honey, please."

"Fuck you!"

"Susan, stop it. It's Tara! Will you just listen to me, for crying out loud."

"Fuck you!"

"Susan, we're trying to help you. . . ."

"Fuck you both!" And she slammed down the receiver.

*   *   *

Later, after an hour's fitful sleep, Susan woke, and a horrible thought presented itself.

It had used Harriet's voice and Harriet was dead. It had used Tara's voice as well.

Shuddering, Susan reached for the phone. If she could speak to Tara, to the real Tara, and assure herself that she was unharmed—

But it would expect that, surely.

She let her hand drop short of the phone.

She lay there, half awake, her mind trying to sort it out. (Whoever she called, wouldn't it know? Wasn't it there, inside her phone, waiting? Could any phone be trusted?)

Still unclear (a weakness was coming over her, of limb and mind, a succumbing to a dread she couldn't resist) she decided to call Maudey; she could tell her if Tara were all right.

She lifted the phone.

"If you want to know about me, Susan, why didn't you just ask me?" Tara's voice said before she could dial. "Why go behind my back?"

"Oh, God, don't do this to me. . . ."

"We're not trying to do anything to you. We're trying to help you."

Susan lay back on the pillow, the phone still to her ear, her eyes filling with tears.

"Did you kill Tara?" she wept.

"Honey, this *is* Tara. . . ."

"Did you kill her, too?"

"You know my voice, honey."

"Have you no pity? No decency?"

"Susan, stop it and listen to me. Come back to town. Harriet and I can help you . . ."

"Our father, which art in heaven, hallowed be . . ."

"Don't do that, Susan, please."

". . . Thy kingdom come, thy will be done on earth . . ."

"Susan, that's not going to help either of us."

". . . Give us this day our daily bread, and forgive us . . ."

"Susan, if you don't stop that, I really will have to hang up."

". . . As we forgive those who trespass against us . . ."

"I'm not kidding, Susan. Stop that!"

". . . Lead us not into temptation but *deliver us from evil* . . ."

"Look, I tried to help you, I really did."

"Deliver us from evil!"

"Susan . . ."

". . . For thine is the power and the kingdom and the glory forever . . ."

"I'll call you later. When you've pulled yourself together."

It hung up, leaving her weeping for two slain friends instead of one.

21

It was useless to run—Susan understood that now. She was safe, for the moment, here in the country. (It wanted her in town; otherwise why resurrect Tara and Harriet to lure her back?)

Susan decided to remain at the hotel and wait.

She dined that evening in the hotel dining room, choosing a table far off in one corner overlooking the pond. She searched the darkness for the ducks but saw only the black, unbroken surface of the water. The room itself was charming (a little solace in that). The furniture was uniformly wicker from the twenties. ("Lou, at least ask your mother if she wants to get rid of the wicker chaise." "You know her—if I ask, she'll carry it over here herself, on her back, and lay it at the feet of her sacred daughter-in-law." "So? Sounds good to me.") Scenes from her past played out in her mind as Susan waited for the waitress to bring her dinner. ("Say *Grammy*, Andrea. Say *Grammy*." "Grammy." "She did it, Susan! She called me Grammy!")

There were few diners in the room—a middle-aged couple with a younger man, finding difficulty in conversation, a mother and daughter arguing quietly (did mothers and daughters always argue? Would she and Andrea?), a single man, youngish, across the room in another corner. He glanced briefly at Susan and then away.

She ate heartily (it amazed her that in the midst of horror she was voracious—a learned Jewish response to horror?).

And then, bloated and sleepy, she decided to circle the pond before going to bed.

Halfway around it, she saw the shadowy figure of a man coming in her direction. She turned, hurrying back to the hotel, but his stride was longer and he caught up to her.

"Beautiful evening, isn't it?"

She looked at him in the spillover light from the hotel porch and recognized the young man from the dining room. The one who had glanced at her. (She had seen the look; brief though it was it had the edge of interest in it.)

"Yes, it is."

"I hope I didn't frighten you, coming out of the shadows like that. I was walking around the pond."

"Yes, so was I."

"Until I showed up," he smiled and in the light of the porch she saw that his smile, like the rest of his face, was handsome.

"I just decided it was too far to walk."

They went inside and he extended his hand toward her.

"Bowen Jessup, or, as my friends call me, the creeper. Sorry I frightened you."

"You didn't. Really."

"I'd rather I did," he said, the boyish smile back in place. "That way I'd owe you a nightcap." He indicated the hotel sitting room, which was empty.

"Not tonight, thank you. I really am too tired."

"Tomorrow, then," he said, as if it were settled. "Sleep well, whatever your name is."

"Susan Reed."

"Sleep well, Susan Reed." And he left her and took a seat, reaching for a yachting magazine on a coffee table in front of him.

Susan climbed the flight of stairs to her room, her cheeks burning slightly at the encounter. It had been years since anyone had tried to pick her up; she hadn't realized she missed it.

She lay on her bed fully clothed, thinking about the young man (at least five years her junior, perhaps more). She enjoyed the way he'd accepted her refusal—his matter-of-factness about it, even to a hint of rudeness in the way he sauntered away, readily accepting the company of a magazine when denied hers. Quite a cock-of-the-walk, this Bowen Jessup.

And quite attractive.

She argued silently with herself. ("I'm not sleepy, not now. Why not go downstairs and have a drink?" "Jesus, Susan, can you really think of anything like that *now*?" "Why not? All rules are suspended in times of calamity.")

Her doubts won, as they always did, and wearily (robbed of an adventure that might have distracted her, at least for a while) she undressed and went to bed.

The phone woke her in the middle of the night.

"Are you feeling any better now?" Tara's voice asked.

"What do you want? Why won't you leave me alone?" Susan pleaded sleepily.

"How can I do that? I'm your friend. I want to help you."

"My friends are dead. You killed them."

"No, Susan, you've got it all wrong. Please, honey, let Harriet and me talk to you."

"Harriet's dead."

"No, she isn't. She's right here with me. Hold on, you can talk to her."

A hesitation and then—"Susan? Honey, it's Harriet."

"You're despicable."

"She's doing it again. Susan . . ."

"Don't call me any more or I'll have the phones removed. I'll go somewhere where there are none. Don't call me again."

And she hung up.

The next morning, Susan sought out Bowen Jessup. (She awoke furious: furious at Lou for having forsaken her; furious at the thing for using Tara and Harriet the way it did; furious at a world wherein such wretched abuses were possible.)

She inquired at the desk (he was not in the dining room for breakfast) and was told that he had gone out for a drive but was expected back.

Following his example, Susan got in her car and drove. Hardly noticing her surroundings (she thought only of him, of what might happen between them, of what she might allow to happen) she returned to the hotel in time for lunch.

He was there, at his same table.

"Good afternoon," Susan said, walking up to him brazenly. "I'll have that drink now, if you don't mind."

He smiled, sure of himself. "How about lunch first?"

"I'd love it." She sat opposite him.

(She recalled, momentarily, that she had been the aggressor with Lou, too, years before.)

They chatted (it was easy with him, he was a master at seduction, Susan decided) about many things, mostly him. Bowen Jessup (the Third, he admitted as if it were in itself amusing) was a stockbroker, single, taking a brief holiday from New York City before settling down to take charge of some troublesome merger of his brokerage house with another (she could barely follow that part of it).

He had, until recently, been living with a black high-fashion model, over whom he and his family ("Bowen Jessup the Second?" she had asked. "No, that was Granddad. The current patriarch is Winston Jessup." "How appropriate," and she had laughed) had several scenes, the most recent being the night before he left town.

The holiday, then, was a flight (like hers) from troublesome responsibilities.

"What about you, Susan Reed?" Bowen said, refilling her wineglass. "Are you going to remain a woman of mystery, or will you tell me something about yourself?"

"Where shall I start?" And she felt the warmth and fuzziness of the wine hit, blessedly. (An afternoon of distraction; a moment off from the inevitable.)

"Why not with your wedding ring?"

Susan glanced down at it and instantly decided to create a character for herself. Better to hide within someone else, for a while, before being called back (literally) to who she was and what she faced.

"The last vestige of my widow's weeds," she lied, killing Lou (a tinge of old, familiar guilt).

"I'm sorry."

"Thank you. It's been a while. I'm over it," and she spun her fantasy, all the while looking nervously into Bowen's startlingly blue eyes. She was, to him, an artist, having just finished a mural (why not? it was her fantasy), needing to get away, to renew herself. She was unattached (*fair game*, she could almost hear him think) and could return to town any time she tired of her whim to see colonial America.

Having thus established themselves (she wondered if he, too, were lying), their conversation turned to art, of which Bowen knew a great deal, theater, of which he knew surprisingly little, and eventually, not surprisingly, to love. (She recalled a dozen such conversations in her past; the young men had always led her to their beds by way of talking of past affairs.)

"I never did fully understand my feelings about Hannah" (his high-fashion model). "I suppose we lived with each other for a lot of wrong reasons."

"Such as?" And Susan sipped the port he insisted they order.

"Outraging the system, for one thing. You should have seen Winston Jessup's face when I brought her home for the weekend."

"I can imagine."

"No, anything you'd imagine is wrong. He didn't even flinch. Just took it all in his stride. Both he and Mother were utterly charming the whole time. Charming and witty and on the verge of complete hysterical tantrums, which, as I knew they would, exploded after we'd gone. I received a letter from dear old Dad, well, more a document than a letter . . .''

Susan wondered at the age of this man whose parents' approval was still important to him (as hers weren't? she chided herself).

"In it, he *decreed* that if I wanted to squander myself on someone unbecoming a *Jessup*, he and Mother would accommodate by no longer considering me one. Nice, huh?"

"To the point." And Susan decided on thirty. "What did they say when you told them you and Hannah had split up?"

"Nothing. I haven't told them. Our affair was none of their business, our breakup isn't either."

Perhaps thirty-five.

They finished their glasses of port and Bowen suggested they take that overdue walk around the pond. They did, and by the halfway mark, Bowen had placed his arm around Susan, who thought perhaps he was in his late thirties after all.

They spent the better part of the afternoon together, walking, a brief drive to a local antique store, back to the hotel and a game of cards. Then they agreed to dine together that evening and Susan went upstairs to her room to do battle with herself.

There was no doubt that she wished to spend the night with Bowen, no doubt and little surprise. (She had never before been unfaithful to Lou; it had not even occurred to her, except in flights of self-indulgent fantasy.) But here it was. And the guilt (there was guilt, but in her disoriented state, it seemed far off, as if it belonged to someone else— someone she had once been?) faded. She bathed, slowly, luxuriously, looking at her body as if she had not seen it in a long time, dreamed as she lay in the hot water of what kind of lover Bowen would be (she promised herself to go through with it). Then, still damp, she slid beneath the bed's covers and tried to nap.

In the warm, vague moments before she fell asleep, she smiled at the thought that there was still pleasure possible, even in these times.

And in his room, Bowen picked up his phone and spoke without dialing.

They made love that night, if indeed you could call it that. (Susan did not.) Suddenly and violently, Bowen was inside her. And just as suddenly, he withdrew. His animal thrusts were painful; he seemed instantly aroused, quickly sated.

She lay there, still winded from the attack (it was more an attack than a sexual act) remembering other times, long ago, when such things had happened to her. But they were at the hands of inexperienced boys, too excited to function normally; this was different. Failure of this sort from a grown man was unexpected and frightening.

"I'm sorry," he said, from the darkness next to her.

"That's all right."

"No, it isn't. And I am sorry."

"Bowen, we hardly know each other. You can't expect either of us to be at our best."

"You're very kind, and at the risk of sounding like a fool, I'd like to say that nothing like this has ever happened to me before."

"Really? You're lucky. It happens to me all the time." She tried to lighten his mood.

"You *are* kind," and he kissed her gently. "I promise, it won't happen again."

Susan was suddenly embarrassed and suggested they leave his room and have a game of Scrabble in the sitting room below.

They dressed but before they were out the door, his phone rang.

Bowen answered it casually enough, although Susan thought she saw a hint of hesitation in his manner.

"Yes?" he said, turning his back to her.

Susan stood there, by the door, uncertain of whether to remain or precede him out.

"Hi . . . that's right . . . uh-huh. . . ."

It was awkward standing there, trying not to eavesdrop, aware that Bowen was answering in monosyllables, his back to her on purpose.

"All right . . . yes, do. Goodbye." He hung up the phone.

As he turned to her, Susan was sure she did see a look of discomfort on his face.

"That was Hannah," he said, and for the moment she believed him.

And Lou and the guilt, each more real now, returned.

They played Scrabble for over an hour, nearly finishing a bottle of anisette that Bowen ordered. And when, finally, he defeated her (she was delighted, it meant they could stop playing), Susan could barely get to her feet.

"Good heavens," Bowen said, taking her arm "are you as drunk as all that?"

"I guess I am. Anisette isn't my drink."

"Want some air?"

"Yes, please." And she stood there, unmoving.

"Want me to bring it to you?"

Susan laughed and followed him outside.

The air was cool and it brought her around.

"I am sorry. You must think I'm some kind of dypsomaniac."

"Tomorrow night we'll stick to wine." He walked with her toward the black pond, arm around her waist.

"Susan, can I ask you something?"

"Yes."

"Will you spend the night with me?"

She didn't answer at first, remembering the clumsiness and painfulness of his lovemaking.

"I'm afraid I wouldn't be much good at it," she said. "Not after all that anisette."

"Just sleep next to me. I promise, I won't ask any more."

There was an air of defeat about him at that moment that Susan assumed was embarrassment over his premature orgasm.

"I warn you, I snore," she said.

"So do I." And he steered her toward the hotel.

Bowen was a man of his word. Lying there next to him, hearing him snore relentlessly, Susan felt the warmth of his body, and the loneliness which had plagued her for so long ebbed.

*   *   *

The next morning Susan awakened to find Bowen's lips on hers.

"What are you doing?" she asked groggily.

"I'm a morning person." His hand cupped her breast.

They made love and it was better this time. But still not good. Bowen was gentle with her and in control, but if anything, he had moved too far in the other direction. His lovemaking seemed emotionless to her, forced in its restraint, lacking all spontaneity.

When it was finished (the chore done, Susan felt) he turned to her.

"Better?" he asked.

"Perfect," she lied.

They breakfasted on the road, Bowen anxious to do some heavy-duty sightseeing—and see the sights they did. He had found out about Sturbridge Village and they spent several hours in the reconstructed colonial village, marveling at everything, spending much too much money on artifacts and souvenirs that would shortly be uninteresting. Then a search of the area for antique shops, boutiques, country stores. Bowen seemed obsessed with his quest for the charming and unusual, and Susan, exhausted, followed at his heels, the perfect female "good sport."

It was after four in the afternoon that her patience and her feet gave way.

"Whoa, no more," she said.

"Just the candle shop in Brearly and then back to the hotel," he said, in charge behind the wheel.

"Bowen, I've got a right foot that's definitely in some kind of trouble and a left I'm sitting *shivah* for."

"What's sitting *shivah*?"

"It's a Jewish wake, which is what you'll be at if you don't get me back to the hotel."

"Two minutes in the candle shop?"

"Two days at my wake?"

"Spoilsport." And he turned the car around.

They arrived at the hotel after five, in darkness, and Susan declined Bowen's offer of (almost insistence on) a glass of port, agreeing to meet him in the dining room for dinner in an hour. (She pleaded for seven-thirty and lost.)

Upstairs, she showered, hoping it would wake her (it didn't), lay down for a while, got up, dressed, cursed the fact that she was involved with a grown boy scout who viewed his trip (and now, hers) as one extended hike, and went downstairs to the dining room.

"Bubbly?" Bowen lifted a bottle of champagne and filled her glass as she sat down.

"Champagne? What are we celebrating?"

"Each other."

She felt an immediate guilt; whatever Bowen felt for her, she didn't reciprocate. It wasn't the sex—that could be overlooked, overcome. No, the simple, cruel fact was that she was using this young man. Using him to assuage her fears, to revenge herself upon Lou, to distract herself.

This new role, that of selfish wanton, was as dissatisfying to her as the old one, the "little woman."

"That's very sweet, Bowen," she said, and, lifting her glass she added, "To you and to your finding what you want."

"I think I just did," he answered, smiling.

Guilt upon guilt.

They ate a celebratory dinner (Bowen had ordered in her absence game hens *à l' orange* and all the possible trimmings) and finished the champagne.

Susan's head spun from the sweetness and the alcohol.

"Two brandies," he told the waitress.

"No, really, Bowen, I've had enough to drink."

"Brandy's good for you. Settles the stomach."

"It would take a Mack truck to do that."

"Two brandies." And the waitress left, envying Susan her strong companion.

They chatted. (Bowen chatted. Susan sat there, obediently staring at his mouth and sipping the brandy, feeling worse.)

Afterward, over the Scrabble board, she felt distinctly nauseated and mentioned it.

"Anisette will cure that." Bowen signaled for the proprietor.

"God, Bowen, the one thing I don't need is another drink."

"Trust me. Anisette is used in commercial preparations as a stomach tranquilizer."

"How do you know that?"

"I come from a long line of alcoholics. Dear old Winston bends the elbow every night from six to eleven and Mother's right there, keeping up with him. There's nothing about the properties of hard liquor I don't know."

Despite herself, Susan agreed to the anisette and dutifully sipped it, encouraged, if not forced, by Bowen.

Mercifully the Scrabble game was a short one.

"Feel any better?" Bowen asked, arranging the tiles in the box.

"Not really. I think it's the sack for me."

"Nonsense. A little drive in the night air will fix you up."

"I don't think so. . . ."

"Susan, trust me. Ten minutes in the cool night air and you'll feel like going dancing."

"Dancing? God, Bowen, give an old lady a break and let me crawl into my bed."

"Just ten minutes."

"Not tonight."

"Please? Ten minutes and then I promise, you won't see me until dawn tomorrow. Please?"

She acquiesced grudgingly, out of guilt (he wanted her company so much more than she his), and shortly found herself in the car, both nauseated and exhausted. The combination of the day's activity and the liquor had been overwhelming. Had Bowen set out to make her ill on purpose he could not have done a better job.

"Lean back and close your eyes," Bowen said as they drove along a dark road. "A little nap will fix you up."

She did, and soon fell into a deep sleep.

Waking (she had no idea how long she'd slept), Susan found that they were driving on a deserted highway.

"Where are we?"

"Hey, sleeping beauty, you're up."

She glanced at the dashboard clock and saw that it was after one.

"My God, why didn't you wake me?"

"I ran out of dynamite. By the way, you do snore."

"Yes, I know. Where are we?"

"On the way to the hotel. I got us lost for a while till I stumbled onto the Massachusetts Turnpike, God bless it. Incidentally, who's Tara?"

"What?"

"You also talk in your sleep."

"I do?"

"Yes, indeedy."

"You're kidding."

"No, you rambled on for quite a while. You seemed to be having an argument with her. Who is she?"

"Just a friend," Susan answered, disturbed. She had not been aware that she talked in her sleep; it had never happened before, to her knowledge. But why would Bowen invent it?

A feeling of dread, as yet far off, stirred in her.

"Can we have some music?" she asked, to avoid the subject.

Bowen complied and they drove without speaking.

She wondered why this revelation that she talked in her sleep was so upsetting to her. It was like finding out a new facet of one's personality that had always been apparent to others—a quirk one didn't like.

She glanced over at Bowen, whose face was set now in a look of utter concentration. What was he thinking about?

She shivered slightly and wished they would get to the hotel soon. She would sleep alone tonight. Tomorrow night as well. This thing with Bowen was getting out of hand. He was controlling her against her will—the endless shopping expedition, the countless glasses of wine and anisette, and now, this unwanted drive. She was better off alone.

"Unhappy?" Bowen asked.

"Groggy, that's all."

"Take another nap."

"Won't we be back soon?"

"There's time for a nap."

Again, his unsolicited advice. Susan leaned her head against the car window, rolling her resentment around in her mind like a newly found thought, examining all sides of it. Bowen, Lou, Yuri, her father, all men were so free with their unasked-for advice to women. So damned dominating. If women did it, they were castrating. With men, it was their sovereign right. Their maleness. She thought back on the night she had met Bowen, his insistence that she have a drink with him, his annoyance that she refused. Would he have felt that way if she were another man? No, surely not.

Feminism über alles, she thought wearily, closing her eyes.

And the dread started to surface.

Two days of being manipulated by Bowen were enough. She had left one dominating male only to find another. No, none of them were any good to her. Not now. Now she was too weakened to fight them off, too abused to pay the price for their protection. If they *could* protect her from the thing that wanted her.

Two *women* had tried to protect her. They were both dead. Soon she would be, too.

She opened her eyes against the thought and looked over at Bowen. His face was still hard-edged in concentration. What *was* he thinking about?

"A penny for your thoughts," she said.

He smiled immediately, hiding whatever they were. "Nothing in particular."

"Come on, tell."

"All right. I never met a woman who talked in her sleep before. I was just wondering about it."

"Why? Does it make me bizarre?"

"No more than usual."

"Very funny." *I don't talk in my sleep*, she thought.

"I knew a chap who did at Princeton. I always thought it was a male phenomenon."

"Sexist. We women are allowed all the perversions these days. Haven't you heard?"

Princeton? Hadn't Bowen said he went to Yale?

"So I've noticed."

Susan glanced out the window and saw the black woods beside the highway, the darkened houses far off, now and then a lighted window, another car on another road.

He did say he went to Yale. She remembered wanting to ask him if he knew an old friend of hers; she hadn't because of the possible age difference. (It was important, then, to hide the fact that she was older than he.)

Bowen was lying. But why? Had he, like her, invented himself?

Again she stared out the window at the highway, deserted now except for them.

"What about that nap?" Bowen said.

"Not in the mood."

"Suit yourself." Was that irritation in his voice?

"We'll be back soon. I can wait."

"We're still a way off."

She saw the roadside reflectors beside the car, passing quickly, too quickly. She glanced over at the speedometer. Seventy.

"You're going to get a ticket."

"You want to get back to the hotel quickly, don't you?"

"Another minute or two won't matter."

"As you wish." He eased up on the accelerator.

It *was* irritation in his voice.

Susan continued to stare out the window, herself growing irritated at his imagined assault on his dominance. His sacred male dominance.

A mileage sign read 97. Ninety-seven miles to what?

The music on the radio was saccharine; she leaned over and changed the station.

Ninety-six. Then, in a very short time, ninety-five. She glanced at the speedometer again. Seventy-five.

Yes, he would have to speed up again. That was what Lou would have done. Painfully predictable.

Why had he lied about Princeton? Yale, Princeton, what was the difference?

Ninety-four.

The dread welled up.

Why were they in the car at all? Why hadn't he let her go to her room when she complained of feeling ill? Why that look on his face, sitting there behind the wheel, petulant and preoccupied?

A sign up ahead caught Susan's eye. She waited until they drew close enough for her to read it.

Hudson. Catskill.

She recalled having passed those towns on her swing into Massachusetts. *Before reaching the turnpike.*

The dread, fully realized now, caught her unaware and she found herself out of breath.

They weren't on the Massachusetts Turnpike as he

had said. This was the New York Thruway. Just ninety-three miles from New York City, where the thing with Tara and Harriet's voices waited for her.

Waited for Bowen to bring her to it!

As if in agreement, a small sign flashed by her window.

South.

Her mouth dry, still breathless, Susan closed her eyes, feigning sleep, trying to plot against the messenger beside her.

Of course—that was why Bowen was incapable of making love; incapable of any show of tenderness.

She had to get out of the car.

Again, the signs tried to help her.

Gas. Food. Two miles.

"Can we stop up ahead?" she tried and succeeded in sounding casual.

"Hungry?" the messenger asked.

"No, dear. Much more basic."

They drove in silence except for the lush music coming from the radio. Then, up ahead, she could see the service station and restaurant pull off.

"Would you get coffee while I freshen up?" She attempted coyness to cover her fear.

"Uh-huh," the messenger said.

They pulled into the parking lot. Bowen turned off the ignition, putting the car keys into his right jacket pocket.

They crossed the dark empty lot together.

No other cars in which to escape.

Inside the ladies room, Susan tried to think. She could run to the woods, ask the gas attendant for help, the waitress, the manager.

But no, she needed the car.

His *right jacket pocket*.

Bowen was at the cash register with two containers of coffee when she reached him.

"Light with sugar, right?" He handed her a Styrofoam cup.

"Yes." She uncapped it. There was steam coming from the hot liquid. Good.

She held it in her right hand and let her left hand brush against his jacket.

"What about brownies, big spender?" she said. "Can we have two of them?"

As the cashier, tired and forlorn, reached for them, Susan let her fingers dip into the messenger's pocket.

"What are you doing?" He looked down at her hand as it closed around the keys.

She screamed, in part to release the impossible tension she felt, in part to catch him unaware.

She hurled the hot coffee into his face and started to run toward the revolving door, the keys digging into her palm.

As she reached the car, she could see him coming out of the restaurant, running toward her.

"Susan!" he screamed at her. "Don't do this!"

She locked the doors from the inside and fumbled with the keys, trying to insert the right one into the ignition.

"Susan, let me talk to you!" The messenger was at the door, trying it.

One key refused entry. She tried another.

"Susan, please let me explain. You've got it all wrong."

The key, the right one, slid into its slot and she pumped the gas pedal.

"Susan, for God's sake, don't do this!"

He was pounding at the window, trying to break it.

"Listen to me! Just listen to me!"

She shifted into drive.

"I'm trying to help you, don't you know that?"

As she sped away, she saw the messenger in the rear-view mirror, cursing and stamping his feet.

22

Susan reached the hotel shortly before three in the morning. Its front door locked, she woke the proprietor, made a hasty excuse about a car accident ("Mr. Jessup is in the hospital; I'm leaving to join him") and hurried to her room to pack.

The phone rang as she closed her suitcase.

"Susan? It's Tara. Can you spare me a minute?" The thing was angry now.

"What do you want?"

"First of all, I must say, I think you're behaving very badly."

"Am I?" And the ludicrousness of it made Susan laugh. "Yes, I suppose I am."

"Poor Bowen was just trying to help you."

"I was right then."

"About him, yes. About everything else, no. You're reacting like a child, Susan. At least let

Harriet and me sit with you, explain it all to you, that's all we ask.''

"That's all?"

"Of course that's all. Look, get in the car and meet us at my apartment.''

"Why? Why don't you come here if you want to talk to me so badly?''

"It's impossible. Honey—" and the thing softened its voice—"trust me. You know everything I've done for you in the past. I'm not going to desert you now.''

"Why do I have to come to New York?"

"That's just the best way, Susan.''

"Why?"

"It just is.''

"Why?"

A hesitation, and then, "Coming back would be a sign of acceptance—of your willingness to join us.''

"To *join* you?"

"Of course. No one is taken against his will, Susan. All that nonsense about atrocities is . . .''

"To *join* you? Jesus God Almighty . . .''

"Susan, calm down . . .''

"You think I'd ever *join* you?"

"You're not going to get hysterical again, are you?''

"You must be insane! You must be . . .''

"Susan, if you don't stop these unwarranted attacks on me, I'm not going to be able to help you at all.''

"Insane! . . .''

"Susan . . .''

"You vile, unspeakable . . .'' She was crying now.

"Susan, I'm losing patience with you.''

"Monster!"

"Just who do you think you're talking to?" the thing asked.

"God, stop this horror!"

"Nobody's going to stop anything unless I say so."

"Boruch atah adonoi elohaynu . . ."

"Susan, stop that this minute."

". . . Melech haolom . . ." She searched her memory for the rest of her childhood Hebrew prayer, but it remained out of reach.

"Not another word of that gibberish, Susan."

"Boruch atah adonoi elohaynu melech . . ."

"Susan!"

"Boruch atah adonoi . . ."

"You idiot, stop it!" And then the voice changed, darkened, deepened. It was no longer Tara but the unspeakable rasp she had heard long ago. "You little bitch!"

". . . Elohaynu melech . . ."

"You dirty little bitch . . ."

". . . haolom . . ."

"You have an eternity of eating shit ahead of you."

". . . elohaynu melech haolom . . ."

"Did you hear what I said, bitch?"

". . . boruch atah adonoi . . ."

"You'll rim me until Armageddon on your knees . . ."

". . . boruch atah adonoi . . ."

"I'll fuck you bloody!" And the voice disappeared. In its place, the Silence, more powerful than ever.

Susan's entire body shuddered and went into spasm at its sound. As she fought the receiver back onto its cradle, sweat dripped from her hair, a wave of nausea gagged her, she felt her bladder release its contents.

Thus degraded, soiled and terrified, Susan clutched her suitcase and fled.

She drove east for hours along the darkened turnpike, the real Massachusetts Turnpike this time, ignoring her tiredness and her terror.

No one is taken against his will.

Would that protect her? Or would the thing grow angry enough to break its own rules and take her without her consent?

A new thought, even more frightening, occurred to her: Could the thing truly torture her into accepting the ultimate horror? Was there any pain worth that?

Dawn was rising now ahead of her, the sky lightening from black to blue, reminding her that she had missed a night's sleep. The tiredness was deep; several times the car edged its way to the shoulder of the road only to require a new spurt of energy to center it.

She needed sleep desperately. As much for her mind as her body.

As the sky lightened to gray, she saw an exit up ahead. She took it and blessedly found a small motel near the turnoff. It was almost seven in the morning by the time she reached the motel door and found it locked. Inside, she saw the pale-yellow light of a lamp and knocked.

Presently a woman, shaking off the remnants of her own tiredness, came to the door.

"Been driving all night?" the woman asked as Susan wearily signed the register.

"Yes, I'm afraid I have."

"Well, you've come to the right place. We have the softest beds in the area, if I do say so myself. Frank Roos wouldn't have it any other way. That's my husband. He died last year."

"I'm sorry," Susan said, reaching for her suitcase.

"He was a perfectionist, you know. Everything had to be just so. I suspect that's what killed him. Too much expectation, not enough satisfaction. Now you take me, I'll live forever. It all rolls off my back like a duck. Here, dear," and she handed Susan a key. "That's the way to take life. Nice and easy. You're in number fourteen. Frank did it in green, nice and restful. You look like you could use a good night's sleep."

"Yes." Susan started toward the door.

"Well, then that's the right room for you. Frank always liked to suit the guest to the room. There's more to running a motel than most people give you credit for . . ." and her words trailed off.

Inside room fourteen, Susan wearily removed her shoes and lay on the bed, fully dressed.

Her eyes burned as she closed them. She was aware that her dress was soiled. Had she been less exhausted, she would have showered, but now even removing her clothes was too much for her.

She lay there, waiting for sleep.

She saw Bowen reflected in his car's rearview mirror, cursing at her, a fist upraised.

And the thing's true voice.

I'll fuck you bloody!

And Andrea, watching her mother go.

She turned on the bed, reaching for a second pillow, trying to find a position that would allow sleep.

She saw the ambulance in front of the telephone building in the city and heard someone on the street say a woman had been killed.

And again, Andrea, alone.

She turned again, hugging the pillow now, trying to force sleep.

She heard a sound.

A soft whirring noise.

Her eyes, welded shut, burned as she thought of opening them.

The sound continued.

She was deeply, profoundly tired. She lay there, not wanting to hear it, not wanting to deal with anything but the need to be asleep.

It continued, softly.

Susan turned toward it, slowly, any movement requiring enormous effort, effort she could not tolerate.

She willed her eyes to open but they refused.

A turning. A low, almost inaudible turning.

She remembered stepping over locusts in her apartment in another lifetime, and her eyes opened.

And focused.

There, across the room on a dresser was a phone, the mouthpiece of which slowly turned, unscrewing itself.

She watched it as if under water, feeling nothing, drugged from exhaustion.

The black plastic mouthpiece made one final turn and fell to the dresser top.

And the small metal speaker after it.

They lay there, quivering, then motionless.

And then, from the hole in the receiver, came a snake.

It slowly glided out, black, glistening, perhaps four feet long in all, its permanently open yellow eyes searching the room for Susan.

Their stares met; Susan's face displayed nothing (it was too late for fear now, only recognition was possible), the snake cocked its head toward her, showing its black, rubbery smile.

It slid across the top of the dresser, first to one end, then to the other, looking for a way down, down and across the room to the bed.

Susan stared, motionless, fascinated, drugged.

It opened its black mouth, still smiling, and showed its fangs proudly. A tongue, also black, flicked at her across the room, and then, turning, the snake undulated up the wall, fell back to the dresser, and continued its search.

It was the memory of Andrea that brought Susan round; the memory of the day in the country when, upon seeing a snake, the child had burst into tears.

Susan moved to the edge of the bed and slowly let her feet slide down to the floor and to her shoes, staring at the snake all the while, lest it suddenly find its route to her. The shoes on, she reached for her purse on the night table beside her.

Seeing it, the snake hissed and the fangs once again caught the light.

It coiled.

Walking around the bed would bring Susan closer to it; she lifted her legs and rolled to the far side, nearer the door.

It drew its head down; its coiled body shuddered, forcing the poison from its sacs.

It was ready to strike.

Susan leaped for the door and made it. Outside, the door slammed shut behind her, she hurried to her car and, locking herself inside, wept.

And within room fourteen, the snake stared at the closed door with unblinking eyes and then, slowly, returned from whence it came.

Shortly after ten, Susan heard rapping. She opened her eyes to find that she had fallen asleep in the car.

"Are you all right?" the motel owner called through the closed window to her.

Susan opened the door and got out. "Yes, I'm sorry. I guess I fell asleep."

"You poor thing, you didn't even make it to your room."

"No." (She now knew the irresponsibility of telling anyone what was happening to her.)

"You come right with me, young lady. I'll make you some tea."

The kindness, any kindness, overwhelmed her, and Susan started to cry anew.

"Why, what's the matter?"

"Nothing, it's just . . ." (say nothing, explain nothing, think of Tara and Harriet) ". . . I haven't been able to sleep in such a long time. . . ."

"Oh, dear, I know what that's like." The woman took her arm. "I've got something for that, don't you worry."

She led Susan inside the motel to her own small apartment and sat her down in the kitchen.

"When Frank Roos died, I mourned myself into a regular fit, yes I did." She filled a kettle and moved it to the stove. "Did you lose someone, dear?"

"Yes. My . . . sister."

"Oh, now that's hard. Of course, losing any loved one's a misery, but you can't let yourself fall to pieces. She wouldn't have wanted that, any more than Mr. Roos would've wanted me to go on the way

I was. Just fell to pieces. Lay down and didn't want to get up.'' She searched a cupboard drawer, removing odds and ends and piling them up on the countertop.

"Couldn't sleep, couldn't eat, I mean, I was one mess, let me tell you. But you get over it. You have to. Life's to live and mourning's to pass.''

She lifted a prescription bottle from the drawer and held it up to the light to read its label.

"No, this is Mr. Roos's. Well, we won't be needing this any more,'' and she tossed it into the trash and returned to her search.

"Thirty-seven years I was with Mr. Roos, since I was nineteen. He was a bit older but strapping. A strapping man, if you get my intent.'' She smiled naughtily and brought out another bottle.

"Nope, this one's not right, 'less you have arthritis, but I doubt it, at your age.''

"No,'' Susan answered weakly.

"Count your blessings while you've got 'em to count.''

A third prescription bottle was produced and approved. "Here you go.'' The woman put it on the table in front of Susan. "When I had sleeping trouble, Mr. Roos's lodge fellow, Doctor Schechter, gave them to me. He said half a one will make you sleepy, a whole one will knock you out.'' She uncapped the bottle, Susan heard the rattle of the pills, and put one down on the table in front of her. It was pale blue, elongate, divided in two halves by a tiny trench. "I think it's safe to say you're a whole pill customer. You have this with your tea, then we'll get you tucked in good and proper, and see you at dinner time.''

The lie told, Susan was obliged to carry it through.

She took the pill with her tea (she could sleep without it, surely, but the deeper the sleep the better) and watched as Mrs. Roos returned the small bottle to the cupboard drawer and with one sweep of her hand had all the bits and pieces on the counter clattering on top of it.

She allowed the woman to escort her to her room, and even, in her kindness, to help her undress.

"You're very sweet," Susan said, when the covers had been pulled up over her and tucked firmly beneath the sides of the mattress.

"Doesn't cost any more to be nice. Besides, maybe you'll turn out to be one of those philanthropists traveling incognito, giving away a million dollars. I remember a TV show about a man who did that . . ." and she noticed the phone. "People," she snorted. "Why would anybody do that?" She screwed the mouthpiece together as if she were flicking a remnant of dust from the dresser top. "Now you get that sleep, young lady. I'll come in around five and we'll see if you're up to dinner. Mr. Roos used to say I'm not a fancy cook, but what I make sticks to your ribs long after French cooking's out to sea." She turned and smiled on her way to the door. "He was vulgar every once in a while, Frank Roos was. Sleep tight."

"Thank you, Mrs. Roos."

"Bessie."

"Thank you, Bessie."

Alone, Susan fought her way out from under the straitjacketing blankets, crossed to the dresser and placed the phone, now harmless-looking, in a drawer. Then she wedged a chair (a wave of sleepiness hit, the pill was working) against the drawer and went back to bed.

She was asleep in moments.

And dreaming.

"Are you ever going to pass that joint?" Tara asked, sitting in her apartment, which had no walls.

Susan was standing, looking down at the street far below. A man was next to her—a composite of Yuri and Lou. He took the joint from her.

In the street, a taxi pulled up and Harriet got out. Then, in circus-clown makeup, there followed Andrea, Lou's mother, her own mother and even Sweet William with a party hat bobby-pinned to his head. They stood there, looking up at her.

"Mommy, where are the stairs?" Andrea called.

Susan became aware that there were none.

"Tara, why didn't you have stairs put in? All those ridiculous pillows and no stairs."

"Stare at this." Tara held up her middle finger.

Susan glanced over at the man, who was naked. "Stare at this," he said, displaying his erection.

Tara took it in her mouth and Susan looked away.

She was aware that she wanted to leave. She was embarrassed at witnessing Tara and Yuri/Lou's love-making, and Andrea was downstairs waiting for her.

"Mommy?"

"What, darling?"

"Where are the stairs?"

She heard Tara gag behind her and walked into another room, careful not to go too close to the edge where the walls had been removed, specifically to endanger her.

She smelled smoke. Down in the street, the taxi that had brought Andrea and the others exploded into flames; she could see the driver's hand turn black and fuse with the steering wheel.

And far off, the sound of a fire engine.

"I took the elevator," Harriet said, coming into the room. "I have to talk to you."

Susan turned to her and saw the hatred in her eyes.

"Susan, you're a bitch. Tara and I have thought it all over very carefully, and we've decided you're a bitch. You deserve anything that's coming to you."

"*Everything* that's coming to you," Tara said, coming into the room, now naked. "Lou's a marvel. A saint. Only a woman who's sucked a man's cock knows what a saint he is. You don't deserve him, Susan—" and she and Harriet came closer.

Susan knew they meant to throw her off the building.

"I didn't do anything," she said.

"Of course you did. You go around killing people as if they were of no value whatsoever. Your brother, then us . . ."

The fire engine still rang in the distance.

". . . We try to help you and look what we get in return. A cock in the mouth. I ask you, is that the act of a friend?"

"I didn't do anything!"

"No? Tell it to the judge."

"We're all judged sooner or later," Harriet added. "It's your turn now, Susan. It's very simple, dear."

And Harriet and Tara advanced.

They pushed her. As Susan fell, she heard the fire engine in the distance (still too far away to put up a net and save her). She heard another sound, a thumping. She assumed it was her body, hitting against the side of the building as she plummeted to the pavement, as Sweet William had done for her.

I'm going to die, she thought. *I'm going to die!*

And then, the terror of the thought woke her.

She lay there gasping, still hearing the echo of her body hitting the side of the building and the fire engine, far off.

The ricocheting focused first. It was someone knocking on the door of the room.

"Dear? Are you up? It's Bessie," came from outside.

And then the fire engine became the phone, ringing from within the drawer where she had placed it.

The door opened and Mrs. Roos stood there smiling.

"It's almost five. I thought you might like to get up. Otherwise, how will you sleep tonight?"

Susan knew what was going to happen but the residual grogginess from the pill prevented her from acting quickly. She raised a hand to keep the woman from entering.

"I've made some coffee," Mrs. Roos said and then she saw the dresser. "Whatever is going on here?"

"Don't!" Susan's voice came out heavy, hoarse from the drug, devoid of its warning.

"Did you do that?" Mrs. Roos moved to it.

"God . . ."

"Why would you want to do a thing like that?" And she removed the chair.

"Don't!" Susan tried to get up but her legs were wound in the sheets from her dream struggle. "Don't!"

"It can't be for you, can it, dear?" The woman opened the drawer and reached inside.

"No!"

The mouthpiece of the phone exploded and hit her in the shoulder, going clear through it, hurling her across the room and into the wall. She looked at Susan, eyes wide with shock, and she fell, already growing red from the wound.

A wind howled from the receiver, which hung over the open dresser drawer—a wind of hurricane force, steamy hot and humid. The bed covers were blown up around Susan, a corner of the blanket forced halfway down her throat.

A chair was lifted up and smashed into a mirror; the shards exploded everywhere.

The phone itself rose and hovered above the dresser, the receiver flailing wildly beneath it as the wind howled out of it.

Susan fought the blanket from her throat and mouth; she was pressed up against the wall by the force of the wind, her hair standing straight on end, a malevolent halo around her head, which dripped blood from the mirror cuts.

The wallpaper peeled in ribbons around the room and curled down the walls.

She tried to speak, but the wind filled her mouth and threatened to suffocate her.

She crawled to the woman, now unconscious, as the bed was upturned and held against the wall, a full foot from the floor.

The carpeting buckled and came up at the edges, ripped and tore into shreds that flew around the room like green snakes.

Having reached Mrs. Roos, Susan took hold of her arm, slippery with blood, and dragged her, crawling toward the door.

A dresser drawer flung itself at her and knocked her to the floor momentarily.

She was up again, crawling, pulling the bloody burden behind her.

And the phone slowly moved to the center of the room and levitated there, spewing its hot, evil-smelling flatulence.

23

Susan was past New Paltz now, an hour and a half from the city and Andrea.

It was still early, not yet noon, and she knew exactly what had to be done.

The bottle of sleeping pills, eighteen in all, were secreted next to her, in her purse. *("Half a one will make you sleepy, a whole one will knock you out.")*

What would eighteen do?

They would save her. She would be dead before the thing could take her. *Could force her to consent.*

But first she would speak to Andrea. She would tell her how much she loved her, how much the child had added to her life, how proud and grateful she was to have had her.

She would give Andrea a message to hear, over and over again, in the years before the memory of her mother faded, as her own memory of her father had done.

She would hold her beloved once more and then cheat hell itself.

If there was a hell, there was a heaven. She would see Tara and Harriet again.

Happily, not Mrs. Roos. She had been spared. ("No more!" Susan was screaming when the men found her. "No more!" And she fled before the police arrived.)

Oddly, she was calm. Only the unknown had the power to frighten her. And now nothing was unknown.

She even smiled at the thought that everything she had been told as a child was true. All the prayers, all the lore and fables. All true.

It comforted her, as she drove to her death, to know that the universe was a simpler place than man made out of late; there was good and evil, God and hell, love and hate, all balancing one another in an orderly, predictable progression.

To fight was chaos.

To flow with it, order.

Her death would be correct. And in pursuing it herself (no struggle, no denial) she would rid herself of the grotesquery that wanted her.

She would be as free after her death as she was before her birth.

The cosmic rightfulness.

She glanced in the rearview mirror (could the police have followed her from Mrs. Roos's motel?). Only a red van, directly behind her.

She turned on the radio and luckily found Mozart to spend her last hours with. The purity of the music reaffirmed what she had been thinking.

This, then, was her first religious experience, coming as it did at the end of her life. Perhaps she could tell Andrea something of it; something the child could hold to when the world (in her absence) told her there was no meaning to it all.

She was driving across the Harriman State Park, less than an hour from her daughter.

The question of Lou returned. Ought she to see him, too, to say goodbye?

In her present calm she decided she would. Perhaps she could tell him something of the truth she knew, both for his sake and Andrea's. She felt no resentment now; he had turned away from her the way she had turned away from God. There was no fault in either; it was done out of ignorance, not malice.

And three cars behind her. A red van speeded up.

She parked down the block from the school a little after one, and, sitting there for a moment, gathering her thoughts, knowing the last thing she had to do in life would be the most difficult, she fought the desire to weep.

She entered the lobby of the school (the pictures on the walls were different now; she felt no pang of remorse or failure) and went upstairs to Andrea's classroom.

It was empty.

Of course—the children would be at lunch, in the basement cafeteria.

She climbed down two flights of stairs, rehearsing.

("I love you more than anything in the world, Andrea. I've always loved you. I always will. But I have to go away for good now. . . .")

The cafeteria was a hubbub of noisy, happy children and tolerant, if weary, teachers. Susan sought Andrea's face among the hundreds.

She saw her teacher, Candy, dispensing cartons of milk at one of the long central tables and went to her.

"Mrs. Reed," Candy said with obvious surprise. "You're back."

"Yes. Is Andrea here?"

The teacher's face briefly registered concern, then she took Susan by the arm and walked her to the wall, farther from the children.

"She's upstairs with Janet Rasmason."

Nurse Rasmason.

"Why? What happened?"

"Nothing, she's fine. Just upset."

"Why?"

"You'd better see Janet about it. On the second floor, room . . ." But Susan was already hurrying away, between the aisles of boisterous children.

Upstairs, Janet Rasmason's door was closed. Susan rapped softly, and in a moment the young nurse opened it.

"Mrs. Reed, they did reach you."

"No, I was downstairs. What happened?"

The young woman came into the hallway, closing the door after her.

"I was called down to the office about an hour ago. Andrea was having an anxiety attack, as near as I could tell. She was crying, completely incoherent . . ."

"What happened?" Susan repeated desperately.

"Well, that's just it. We're not sure. She got a phone call and when she was brought down to answer it . . ."

Susan heard no more. She covered her face and whispered, "No, please. Don't do this. Not to her. Not to a baby."

*   *   *

Later, when Nurse Rasmason was sure that Susan was in control of herself, she allowed her to see Andrea. The child was sleeping on a cot in her office. Even in her sleep, one could see the effect of the Silence on her. She trembled occasionally, her face contorted from the nightmares she was experiencing.

Susan went to her knees beside the cot and put her arm around her child. She tried to withhold her tears as she whispered. "Shhh, sweetheart. Don't be afraid. Nothing's going to harm you. . . ."

And with her free hand, Susan undid the clasp on her purse and withdrew the small bottle of pills. Still holding and stroking Andrea, she let it fall, with her hopes, into a wastepaper basket.

Later, when Andrea's sleeping face was peaceful (it knew it had won; there was no further need of the child and so it had released her), Susan kissed her daughter and left quickly.

Outside, the red van was parked, its windows tinted black so that no one could see within.

Coming through the door, Susan saw it. And understood.

It was her time to consent.

She looked up at the sky, memorizing it, breathing it in, looking at what was and had always been, the clouds, the sun, the trees, the people.

And she reached for the handle.

NEW YORK, NEW YORK, July 14, 1981—Louis Reed of 312 West End Avenue, Manhattan, has requested that if any of our readers have information as to the whereabouts of his wife, Susan Goodman Reed, now missing from their home for four weeks, they contact him at (212) 555-4733. A substantial reward is offered.

The *Daily News*
New York, N.Y.

Bestselling Books
for Today's Reader